TOURNAMENT OF ALIENS
VISUAL GUIDE

To Brian and Phoebe, whose countless hours and unprecedented dedication have built a world in which all of the mysterious creatures of the universe can mingle with those of us who choose to unlearn everything we know.

Compiled and Edited By:
Chris Corrada
Unbeliever Rus
Unbeliever Carey

Illustrated By:
Chris Corrada
@Jawadog

Research and Writing Team:
Meghan Arnold
Donna Banz
Unbeliever Carey
Lydia Elaine Frechette
Jermaine Hall
Daniel Joseph
Drea Mora
Jude Prestia
Raymond Rowell
Russell Ryan

Special thanks to the families and significant others of the Visual Guide Team who tolerated and supported all of the work that went into this project. We would like to specifically thank Missy Corrada, Christina Ryan, and William, Jack, and Alex Ryan.

Published by The Unbelievable Podcast
Questions, Comments? Please contact unbelievablepodcast@gmail.com

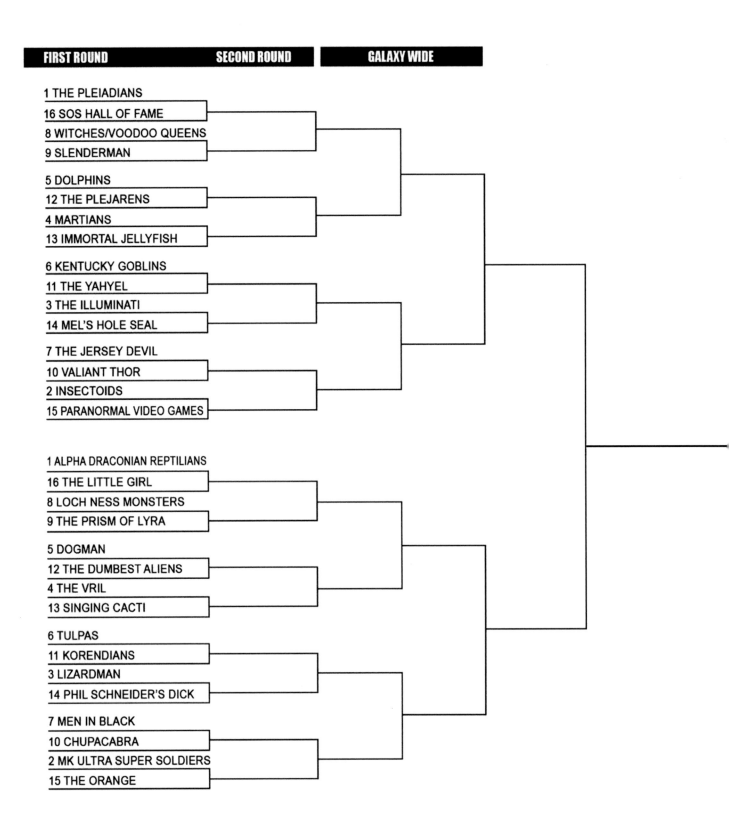

FIRST ROUND

SECOND ROUND

GALAXY WIDE

1 THE PLEIADIANS
16 SOS HALL OF FAME
8 WITCHES/VOODOO QUEENS
9 SLENDERMAN

5 DOLPHINS
12 THE PLEJARENS
4 MARTIANS
13 IMMORTAL JELLYFISH

6 KENTUCKY GOBLINS
11 THE YAHYEL
3 THE ILLUMINATI
14 MEL'S HOLE SEAL

7 THE JERSEY DEVIL
10 VALIANT THOR
2 INSECTOIDS
15 PARANORMAL VIDEO GAMES

1 ALPHA DRACONIAN REPTILIANS
16 THE LITTLE GIRL
8 LOCH NESS MONSTERS
9 THE PRISM OF LYRA

5 DOGMAN
12 THE DUMBEST ALIENS
4 THE VRIL
13 SINGING CACTI

6 TULPAS
11 KORENDIANS
3 LIZARDMAN
14 PHIL SCHNEIDER'S DICK

7 MEN IN BLACK
10 CHUPACABRA
2 MK ULTRA SUPER SOLDIERS
15 THE ORANGE

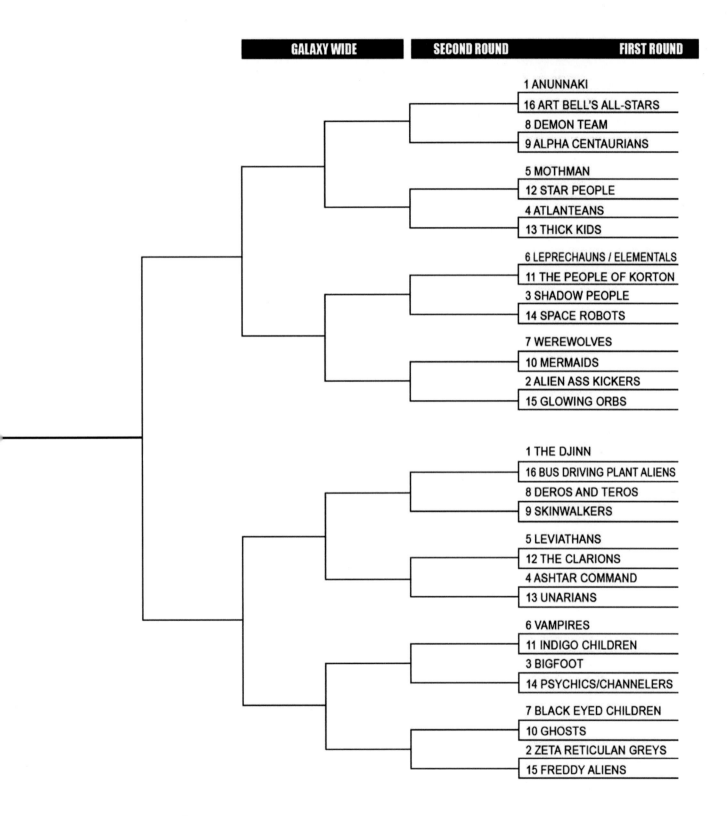

GALAXY WIDE   **SECOND ROUND**   **FIRST ROUND**

1 ANUNNAKI
16 ART BELL'S ALL-STARS
8 DEMON TEAM
9 ALPHA CENTAURIANS

5 MOTHMAN
12 STAR PEOPLE
4 ATLANTEANS
13 THICK KIDS

6 LEPRECHAUNS / ELEMENTALS
11 THE PEOPLE OF KORTON
3 SHADOW PEOPLE
14 SPACE ROBOTS

7 WEREWOLVES
10 MERMAIDS
2 ALIEN ASS KICKERS
15 GLOWING ORBS

1 THE DJINN
16 BUS DRIVING PLANT ALIENS
8 DEROS AND TEROS
9 SKINWALKERS

5 LEVIATHANS
12 THE CLARIONS
4 ASHTAR COMMAND
13 UNARIANS

6 VAMPIRES
11 INDIGO CHILDREN
3 BIGFOOT
14 PSYCHICS/CHANNELERS

7 BLACK EYED CHILDREN
10 GHOSTS
2 ZETA RETICULAN GREYS
15 FREDDY ALIENS

ALIEN ASS KICKERS

Ed Walters (aka Zehass)

Episode 167 & 168: Gulf Breeze UFO's

Strengths: Leg Sweeps, Hiding in trash cans, Quoting George Bush, Sand

Weaknesses: Blue beams, Philip Klass, Floors with urine

Physical Description: White male, Middle age, Readable lips, Slim build

In 1987, wealthy contractor Ed Walters saw a UFO in the small Floridian town of Gulf Breeze that would put the entire nation into a frenzy. Under the pseudonym "Mr. X", Ed submitted many convincing UFO pictures to the local Gulf Breeze Sentinel newspaper. These photos sparked a flurry of interest in UFOs across the country and propelled Walters to fame. Ed's story and photos became so popular that he was featured on the Oprah Winfrey Show where he faced off against famed UFO debunker Philip Klass and uttered the famous line "Read my lips, I've never said that I've been abducted".

Through hypnotic regression, Ed realized that the UFO had hit him with a blue beam and that he had in fact been abducted. His alien abductors referred to him as "Zehass", most likely because their only human friend was named Zehass and they didn't want to seem racist. He was surrounded by 20 aliens and told "12 wait Zehass" and "We know your passion". He began to fight them by throwing sand but ended up biting his own tongue in the process as they continually referred to him as Zehass.

Ed was then approached by one of the aliens and decided it was time for action. Going full Jackie Chan, Walters used his greatest attack: The Leg Sweep! Instead of landing the move, he fell on the alien and came to the realization that they smell like shit. In retaliation, the aliens began beating him over the head with a rod. After the beating, a strange device was placed over his head and he lost consciousness. When he awoke he was in Costa Rica.

Although his first alien battle was a failure, Ed learned from his mistakes. He went on to outsmart Reptilians numerous times by deploying such tactics as garbage can hiding, NHL style shirt pulling over the head, and of course his patented Leg Sweep!

Quotes:

"Read my lips, I've never said that I've been abducted" - Ed Walters

"Zehass 12 wait" - Alien

"I will fight you, I will fight you" - Ed Walters

ALIEN ASS KICKERS

John Titor II

Episode 182: Time Travel Part IV: John Titor
The Second

Strengths: Time travel, Military training,
Alien friends, Tesla Death Ray

Weaknesses: Advanced age, Possibly a liar,
Government controlled

Physical Description: Normal sized human

John Titor the 2nd worked in the Dulce base in New Mexico where human cloning was being done under the guidance of reptilians and grey aliens. He discovered that he was a clone and part of the secret program at the base. While there, he made a grey alien friend named "Rock". John and Rock have a telepathic bond. While John was in training, Rock was brought into the classroom to teach the class to use telepathy. Rock is four feet tall with a very frail body but is chill AF. Rock thinks that humans are funny and his favorite thing to do is watch football with John while eating nacho cheese flavored Doritos.

John was transferred to Wright Patterson Air Force Base where he joined a secret four-man time travel team. Using the TR3B ASTRA time travel vehicle, John and his team traveled to the year 2050 and discovered the world in a state of decline. The Earth is suffering from global famine, extremely high temperatures and dying oceans. In this future, John learned that World War 3 was started in 2018 by Iran and Russia. John's team along with reptilian and grey aliens were able to travel back and prevent it.

John's also learned that the Annunaki would travel back in time to the year 200 B.C. in an attempt to reconquer the Earth by taking over the first empire of China. John's team was able to travel to that time and arm the ancient Chinese with a repeating crossbow with steel-tipped arrows. They were able to defeat the highly advanced Annunaki using Tesla death ray guns and it is because of this that John is included in the "Alien Ass Kickers" team.

Did You Know:

The original John Titor was a time traveler from the year 2036 who traveled to the year 2000 and posted a bunch of stuff on a message board. That's it, that's the story.

ALIEN ASS KICKERS

Kyle Odom

Episode 154: Kyle Odom and the Hypersexual Martians

Strengths: Facebook, Drawing martians, Shooting speed

Weaknesses: Blue Beams, Pamphlets about Jesus, Unemployed, Shooting Accuracy, Old men in grocery stores

Physical Description: Former Marine, Strong, Beefcake, Blonde hair

Kyle Odom shot Pastor Tim Remington in a church parking lot 6 times (and he survived). Kyle then went on the run, hopped on a plane and friended 50 people on Facebook.

He was then arrested in DC as he attempted to throw a manifesto on the lawn of the White House for Barack Obama.

The manifesto detailed what led to the shooting of the pastor:

- He was hit by a blue beam which made college easy and he dropped out
- He couldn't sleep and fucked up a job interview
- A man on a plane made his head hurt, showed him a newspaper article and told him to buy a prepaid cell phone
- He got texts from a church called "The Altar"
- Aliens would sniff him and give him gigantic boners
- He performed oral sex on a bunch of aliens in a grocery store
- He went to Pastor Remington's church and all of the aliens were sniffing him
- Pastor Remington revealed he was a Martian
- Kyle drew a picture of the Pastor and it looked like a Ninja Turtle
- Kyle shot him
- Kyle knew that Obama was also a sex slave

Quotes:

"You are nothing but a toy, your purpose is to now suck our penises" - Old Man (Martian)

ALIEN ASS KICKERS

Phil Schneider

Episode 31: The story of Phil Schneider
Episode 121: Phil Schneider Revisited

Strengths: Walther PPK with a nine shot clip, Shooting aliens, Public speaking, Mutant-like recovery power

Weaknesses: Missing fingers, Split open like a fish, No toenails, Crispy crittered left foot, Cancer, Osteoporosis, Plastic sternum, Multiple Sclerosis, Removed right lung, Metal plate in his head, Tracheotomy, Plastic hip

Physical Description: Big guy with a crew cut and many ailments, visible wounds, and other hardships.

Philip Schneider was an ex-government geologist and structural engineer with 17 years experience working in government black projects who specialized in building Deep Underground Military Bases (DUMBs). His father Oscar Schneider was brought over to the United States of America in Operation Paperclip. Phil had a Rhyolite 38 security clearance and was one of only three human survivors of the August 1979 Dulce Wars. Sixty-six government agents and crack troops lost their lives during this battle. He shot and killed two 7ft tall alien grays with his Walther PPK ("Yes, they are mortal and they do die"). At some point, he spent months at Area 51 working as an interpreter for a reptilian that was captured by the United States government.

His dick was split in half like a hot dog bun (this happened either when he was hit by the alien's blue beam, an infection, or shrapnel from when he was a construction engineer in Vietnam).

The coroner's report on Phil's autopsy overlooked many of his physical ailments among those being the description of his genitalia as "unremarkable". His wife Cynthia, the only woman worthy of Phil's love, noted that Phil's penis was "very" remarkable in that it was sliced down the bottom from tip to back like a hotdog bun. When she was asked to identify his body, she was shocked to see that the corpse had a pristine penis leading her and many others to believe that this body was not the body of Phil Schneider.

Quotes:

"You don't need to pick up a gun to fight for something. You need to pick up your mouth! You need to pick up your brain and read a book!"
– Phil Schneider

"Now, something's wrong here."
– Phil Schneider

ALIEN ASS KICKERS

Captain Kaye (aka Randy Cramer)

Episode 106: The Earth Defense Force and Battling Aliens on Mars

Strengths: High intelligence, Ability to run/climb and shoot, Super soldier training, Immune to germ warfare, Super speed and strength

Weaknesses: Dreams, Age regression, Jawas

Physical Description: White male, Mid 30's with a stubble goatee beard, Shaved head and glasses

Randy Cramer grew up plagued by strange dreams of aliens and would wake up with unexplained bruises and marks on his body. One night Randy had a dream that a four-foot tall cloaked creature that looked like a Jawa was in his dining room. While in spider-man pajamas, he pulled off its hood revealing a box-shaped head with ridged spots covering its bronze-colored face. The creature then lifted him by the arm and genitals which caused Cramer to wake up.

His experience and high test scores caught the attention of the US government and he was included in a secret project called Project Mannequin. He and 299 other children were taught to be super soldiers by playing games like Risk. This training lasted his entire childhood but his memory was suppressed until he was eighteen. At age thirteen he began training with real weapons and live ammunition with SEAL team members to improve his combat skills. He would amaze the special ops soldiers with his ability to run, climb and shoot.

He was physically modified to be fast and strong and received inoculations to protect him from germ warfare. When he was seventeen, he transferred to Project Moonshadow and joined the Earth Defense Force. He spent twenty years protecting the Earth in space and then was age regressed to return to his former seventeen year-old self. After a brief stint on the moon base, Captain Kaye (as he is now known) would be sent to Mars to defend the Mars Colony Corporation Headquarters. His job was to protect the company from alien attack while they extracted valuable mineral resources from Mars.

He killed anything in his way, which makes Captain Kaye a valuable member of the Alien Ass Kickers and a formidable opponent in the tournament.

Quotes:

"What's a Jawa doing in my house?"

"Absolutely, holograms can grab you up by the balls."

ALPHA CENTAURIANS

Episode 131: The Alpha Centaurians Get Laid

Strengths: Seduction, Picking up women,
Interior decorating, Taking babies, Deflecting
rays, Reincarnation, Telepathy

Weaknesses: Human women, Sex addiction,
No weapons, Cockblocking roommates,
Non-aggressive

Physical Description: Tall humanoid with
aquiline features, large grey eyes, and shock
of white hair

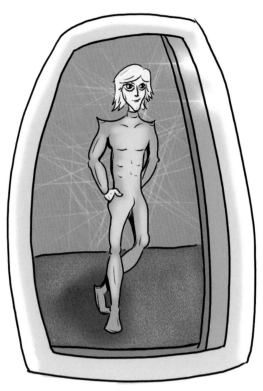

Elizabeth Klarer was born in South Africa in 1910. At age 7, while feeding the
puppies with her sister she saw a UFO. Years later when she was flying with
her Air Force pilot husband she saw a UFO with a great spinning hull and
rainbow colored lights. Her husband's plane had no such lights so she divorced
him.

In 1956, after another divorce, Elizabeth encountered a beautiful alien named
Akon from the planet Meton (part of the Alpha Centauri star system). Eighteen
months later he returned and took her aboard his ship which had glorious rose
red cushy carpeting. Akon's shipmate Sheron was there at the time and
cockblocked them so the two only made out. Soon after their first encounter,
Akon returned without Sheron (Sheron was out picking roots) and the two
made steamy love. Elizabeth reported that the ship had an exoctic green mineral
bath and he gave her a silver ring with magical properties. The ship was a live
organism and the walls changed colors.

At age 49, Elizabeth got pregnant with Akon's baby. Russian Cosmonauts wanted
to capture the alien baby but Elizabeth escaped on a majestic horse. Akon finally
returned for the baby and took Elizabeth up to space for four months.

In Alpha Centauri everything is made of light and energy. The Centaurians only
wear silk. They live in a utopian society where everything is free, everyone is
considerate and gentle and they don't play sports. They live 2000 years, are
non-violent, have no marriage or divorce, and are capable of reincarnation.

Quotes:

"You know, uhh, there's some more
roots I wanted to get on the other side
of the mountain. I shall go and get them
now." - Sheron

"Well, my wife has been in love with a
spaceman for 20 years. That's alright with
me as long as he stays in space where he
belongs." - Elizabeth Klarer's final husband

Alpha Draconian Reptilians

Episode 35: Reptilians vs Palaedians: The Ultimate Battle!

Episode 58: The attack of the Alpha Draconians and the Story of Alex Collier

Episode 96: Reptilians at Hurricane Katrina

Episode 115: Alien Love Bites & The Reptilian Cupid

Strengths: Immense physical strength, Acute instincts, Ability to sense fear, Partial telepathy, Shape-shifting and Dimensional transit

Weaknesses: A small spot in their armpit that allows access to their heart chakra, A hasty leg sweep, Trash cans and Pianos

Physical Description: Towering at 2-3 times the height of a human, the Alpha Draconian Reptilians are scaly reptile humanoids that have varying aesthetics based on their rank in the hierarchy of the race. Attributes can include long tails, wings and yellow or red colored eyes. Of course, as they shape-shift, they could appear to be your President, Queen, favorite pop star or even your parent!

While their official origin is unknown, the Alpha Draconis Constellation is home to this reptilian race where they have since settled to conquer other worlds. Earth is known to be owned by the Alpha Draconian Reptilians where some say the Reptiles live below the Earth's surface. In addition to the subterranean location, they may also live on the moon and on Mars. Many claim they live amongst us in their human shapeshifted form. These aliens feed off of the fear, stress, and general negativity of the human race, believing that any being that is weaker than them deserves to be enslaved. While theory and anecdotal evidence claim they could easily annihilate the human race, they refrain and choose instead to harvest the energy and adrenalized blood of the innocent and infiltrate society by becoming our prominent world leaders and celebrities.

Quotes:

"Do you think blood comes out of Kate Middleton's teet, or..." - Charles Gould

"Al Roker's a lizard" - Brian Frange

ANNUNAKI

Episode 137: LIVE! Definitive Preview of the
Tournament of Aliens, Part I

Strengths: Extremely intelligent, God-like
powers, Extremely long life, Ability to alter
environments and create deadly diseases,
Can create new species

Weaknesses: Human-like emotions like
jealousy, Internal strife due to sibling
rivalry within the species, Slave workers
who revolt or turn into "genetically modified
freaks that just want to fuck kids"

Physical Description: 12 foot tall humanoid,
Very strong, Sometimes referred to as "tall
whites" sometimes referred to as the "black
headed ones", sometimes Aryan, Frequently
depicted wearing bird like masks and crowns

The Annunaki are alien beings from the planet Nibiru, who have a rich and
influential past on planet Earth. We think of the gold rush occurring 150 years ago
with Americans rushing to the uncharted West in hopes to find gold but the history
of the Annunaki suggests that the actual gold rush occurred 450,000 years in the
past, beginning when the Annunaki first visited Earth to harvest gold. Gold became
essential to life on Nibiru, as it could be ionized and used to shield the planet from
the atmospheric damage caused by the Sun's radiation. What began as a mission to
save Nibiru, turned into a millennia-long experiment with a species the Annunaki
created from the DNA of early hominids and their own. These hybrids were created
to be submissive gold digging slaves. Legend has it that these primitive workers
were the origin of the human species that we know today.

According to Annunaki expert Gerald Clark, featured in Episode 90, the Annunaki
are also responsible for using their God-like knowledge and scientific abilities to
create genocide when they've become unsatisfied with their creations and their
procreating habits. He believes this to be the cause for biblical floods and population
altering diseases. Throughout history, the Annunaki have been depicted as ancient
Sumerian Kings, and potentially the basis of other mythological beings.

Quotes:
> "They just walked around pretending
> they were popular! They were just like
> 'oh, look at my feather, I'm a king!'"
> - Phoebe Tyers

"These are people in bird masks
with iPhones." - Brian Frange

THE ASHTAR COMMAND

Episode 109: The Ashtar Command

Members: Ashtar Sheran, Monka, Jesus Sananda, Vrillon, Solganda

Strengths: Interstellar flight, Time travel, Able to negate hydrogen bombs

Weaknesses: Peaceful demeanor, Dependent on fear quotient

Physical Description: 5'6" humanoid aliens with blond hair and a Cuban complection

In 1964, a man named George Van Tassel appeared on Jack Webster's television show and recounted his experiences with the extraterrestrial group known as the Ashtar Command. Van Tassel claimed that a bell-shaped UFO landed on his small desert airport and an alien named Solganda approached him and asked if he would like to see his craft.

The Ashtar Command are from the planet Venus and appear as 5'6" humanoids with a Cuban complexion. The leaders of the Ashtar Command are Ashtar Sheran, Monka, Jesus Sananda, Solganda and Vrillon. Van Tassel channeled these beings for many years and learned the secrets of time travel, $f=1/t$. This knowledge was used to build a machine called the "Integratron", which is like a time machine combined with a Tivo. Van Tassel worked on this machine for 25 years with no success.

The Ashtar Command came to earth to save the human race from the dangers of the hydrogen bomb. They planned on teleporting us to cloned bodies of our younger selves on Uranus in the event of the Earth's destruction. Their message was also broadcast through a famous television interruption where Vrillon spoke directly to viewers about the imminent threat that faced humanity.

Van Tassel passed away in 1978, but their message lived on through channelers such as UFO magazine author Robert Short and Thelma B. Terrell (aka Tuella). Short promised that the Earth would be destroyed and that Ashtar would save those who believed. Tuella continued the message of Ashtar through two books that warned that the Earth would be destroyed magnetically due to the overwhelming negativity on the planet.

Did You Know:

This is The Ashtar Command's second Tournament of Aliens appearance. They were defeated by the Alpha Draconian Reptilians in the third round of the previous tournament.

ATLANTEANS

Episode 34: The Bermuda Triangle and the
        Story of Atlantis

Strengths: Zero point energy, Floating craft,
Ancestors of the Gods

Weaknesses: Flooding, Hubris, Morally
bankrupt

Physical Description: Originally would have
been tall olive skinned humans but have
evolved underwater to be blue skinned
humanoids with gills and webbed fingers.

Atlantis was a grand empire first written about by Plato in 360 BC. It was created
by Demigods and was a wealthy utopian society with a great navy. Plato stated
that his writings were not a myth or warning but rather a true story passed down
by an Egyptian priest. They had extremely advanced technology including
zero-point energy and floating craft. The city was part of Pangaea and suffered a
great cataclysm which caused flooding and destruction some 15,000 years ago. It
is thought that the Atlanteans got arrogant with their advanced technology and
that is what lead to their fall.

Ruins of what could be Atlantis have been found in the Bermuda Triangle off the
coast of Bimini Island. The Triangle is famous for the disappearance of hundreds
of planes and seafaring vessels. These disappearances could be the result of
ancient Atlantean tech like a zero point energy reactor at the bottom of the ocean.
Survivors and witnesses report both UFOs and an electric fog that envelopes
wayward vehicles.

The survivors of the great cataclysm could still be living below the surface or
could have escaped the earth at the last minute in their advanced floating craft. The
beings we call aliens could be the distant relatives of ancient humans who are
now revisiting us because they have a sentimental feeling that this is where they
come from and want to save the earth from suffering the same fate.

Quotes:

"James Cameron is the Illuminati liaison to our underwater allies."
- Crystal Delahanty

Aura Rhanes & The Clarions

Episode 133: Truman Bethurum And Yet Another Hot, Sexy Alien

Strengths: Flying saucers, Rhyming couplets, Making things disappear, Retroscope (view any place in space or time)

Weaknesses: Christians, Peaceful, No weapons

Physical Description: Short, Dark, Sexy, Not Mexican (or Korean), High sing-song voices, Rather odd dress, Berets

One of the first known UFO contactees, in July 1952, Truman Bethurum awoke from a nap during his desert shell-searching expedition to find his truck surrounded by small men between 4 to 8 inches to 5 feet tall. These were the Clarions from the planet Clarion.

Their captain, the unnaturally sexy grandma, Aura Rhanes, then proceeded to engage Truman in a series of baffling yet ultimately fruitless dates. (What a tease!) She has the power to make all flashlights disappear and will decline any photograph requests.

Truman proceeded to see Aura Rhanes everywhere he turned which made him creep out many women in public places by asking if they were aliens.

Quotes:

"You name it!"
- Clarion Greeting

"I expect to be around for a thousand years, but the water in your deserts will be mostly tears." - Aura Rhanes

BIGFOOT

Strengths: Stealth, Large muscular build,
Beautiful blonde hair, Night vision, Speed,
Six fingers on each hand

Weaknesses: Relentlessly hunted, Heart of gold
that just yearns for love

Physical Description: Large, hairy ape-like
creature that smells a little like a skunk. Hair
color varies according to location (Yeti is
white, eastern NC Bigfoot is blonde, Sasquatch
is brown).

Bigfoot is a North-American, ape-like cryptid that lives in forests and is generally
hard to find if sought. Though Bigfoot is mostly associated with the Pacific
Northwest, sightings of similar creatures span the globe.

Bigfoot is a tall, hairy creature, usually averaging 8-10 feet tall. Mostly resembling
an ape, with a few human-like features, bigfoots often leave very large humanoid
footprints bringing many to conclude that it is the missing link to human evolution.

Later sightings of Bigfoot include John Lithgow yelling at a whimpering bigfoot
outside of Seattle, but that can't be confirmed as the evidence was only available
on worn out VHS tapes.

Tim Peeler has had several encounters with Bigfoot, both on camping trips and on
his own property. One day, he bravely faced down a bigfoot that was trespassing
on his property using rough-talking and several punches about the face and belly
with a stick to frighten the beast away from his prized bear dogs and hog dogs.
Peeler claims the police cars that later arrived to the scene frightened the beast
away from further trespassing. He suspects that the bigfoot was attracted to his
property because his dogs were in heat.

Quotes:

"If you've been abducted
by a bigfoot, I wanna hear
about it." - Art Bell

"Bear dogs and hog dogs"
- Tim Peeler

"Get away from here! GIT!"
- Tim Peeler

Black Eyed Children

Ep 137: Live! The Definitive Preview of the Tournament of Aliens Part 1

Strengths: Soul eaters, Can rip out eyes, Creepy appearance

Weaknesses: Have to be invited inside, No real evidence

Physical Description: Small children with pale skin and black eyes

The Black Eyed Children are paranormal creatures that take the form of small children with pale skin and black eyes, usually appearing between the ages of 6 to 16. These creatures have been reported since the 1950's and are mostly sighted as children who are hitchhiking, panhandling or on the doorsteps of a home trying to enter. Often found in Mexico, the Black Eyed Children are believed to be the spirits of murdered children or harbingers of doom.

Most people who encounter these creepy children claim that they use their innocent appearance to try and enter a home or car. They can become very demanding and insist on being invited inside. If invited inside they will eat your soul or rip your eyes out. The easiest defense to these small terrors is to simply not allow them inside. Not much else is known about these creatures whose popularity grew through "Creepy Pasta" stories online. Many believe that these stories are simply an urban legend.

In 2012, a horror film entitled "Black Eyed Children" was funded through Kickstarter. They have also been featured on numerous paranormal television programs. Unfortunately, no evidence other than "friend of a friend" stories has ever been brought forward to prove their existence.

Did You Know

This is the second Tournament of Aliens appearance for the Black Eyed Children. They were defeated by the Pleiadians in the 2nd round of the last tournament.

BUS DRIVING PLANT ALIENS

Episode 128: The Montauk Chair

Strengths: Telepathy, Bus Driving, Ability to see the future

Weaknesses: Thin, Made of plants, Small in size

Physical Description: Small alien made of plants with a slimy green tinge.

Stewart Swerdlow, a survivor of Project Montauk, experienced many frightening abductions as a young child and member of the "Montauk Boys". His earliest memory of these experiences happened when Stewart was only 3 years old. While asleep in his bed, Stewart was taken aboard a bus that was hovering outside of his window. Stewart recalls that the bus was not very large and that his head could almost touch the ceiling of the vehicle.

The only other being with him on the bus was about the same size as his 3 year-old self and was driving the vehicle. This being was not the typical Grey Alien described in books and movies, but rather it had a plant like appearance. The Plant Alien had a green tinge to it and was very thin and slimy. This Bus Driving Plant Alien communicated to Stewart telepathically and somehow let him know, even at 3 years old, that it lived liked a moving plant. The Bus Driving Plant Alien also told Stewart about his future and drove the hovering bus skillfully.

Did You Know:

This is the second Tournament of Aliens for the Bus Driving Plant Aliens. They were defeated in the first round of the previous tournament by The Arcturians.

CHUPACABRAS

Episode 75: Chupacabras, Plum Island, Fairies and the Illuminati

Strengths: Jumping/flying, Sucking blood, Blending into surroundings like a chameleon or the Predator

Weaknesses: A profound lack of goat's blood

Physical Description: Said to resemble a hairless or mangy dog or raccoon. Reptile-like with leathery or scaly greenish-gray skin. They have long, skinny arms and long, skinny fingers, with spines or quills running down their backs.

First sighted in Puerto Rico, Chupacabra translates literally to "goat sucker" after their habit of feeding on livestock, namely goats. What sets them apart from virgin losers like vampire bats and mosquitoes is that the Chupacabra is a porn star and will suck its target completely dry.

Since the original sighting, they have been spotted in several countries throughout Central and South America, along with several reports coming from Mexico and the southern United States. Elusive and rarely photographed or captured, they're mostly evidenced by the dead livestock and pets they leave littered around because they have absolutely no manners.

They also like corn according to a couple in Ratcliffe, Texas who claims to have captured the cryptid after they found it going to town on some corn up in a tree. What they caught pretty much looks like a coyote that may be infected with the parasite Sarcoptes scabiei. There were no goats sucked that night.

The most helpful piece of advice we have now about how to visually identify a chupacabra is that "the most important chupacabra description cannot be trusted." The most convincing accounts come from Central and South America, where they have been described as hopping like a kangaroo and draining the blood of livestock within a concentrated region within the same night or over a series of nights.

Quotes:

"He says he spotted it in a tree, eating corn"

"Raccoon don't make that noise. Or a possum. What makes that noise? I guess a chupacabra does, I don't know."

DEMON TEAM

Strengths: Possession. Cursing entire generations. Causing heart attacks, seizures, insanity, and death. Throwing cast iron soup pots. Having sex with people sleeping.

Weaknesses: Angels. The Holy Bible. Holy water, Palo Santo (holy wood), Phoebe's mom's spiel.

Physical Description: Demons can possess any hot bod they want. Poltergeists are INVISIBLE. No bod; less hot.

Demons have been a plague on the mortal realm since the dawn of time, occupying various forms and disguises besides their own horrifying demon forms. They go by many names but you don't need to learn them because they hate the sound of their own names, and get weirdly pissed off if you say their name.

The sexiest class of demons are the Incubus/Succubus. If they like-you-like-you they will have sex with you in your sleep. This is less fun than it sounds because it typically manifests in the form of sleep paralysis. Incubus is the male sex demon and Succubus is the female sex demon, however, it is likely that they are a non-gender demon that can take on the form of either sex. In order to create demon babies, a Succubus will prey on a human male and once she has collected his seed will turn into an Incubus and impregnate a human female with his demon jizz. There is no Plan B for demonic pregnancies.

Poltergeists were definitely not invented by Steven Spielberg for his 1982 film of the same name (it was called Poltergeist, not Steven). People often call them ghosts, but that's like calling a square a rectangle which is technically correct, but why would you call it that. Poltergeists are the boss level of ghosts. They are wrathful and violent spirits, the angry drunks of the ghost world. Get it, spirits?

Quotes:

"Charles, are aliens actually demons from hell, masquerading as aliens?"
- Brian Frange

"Brian. We gotta get ahold of this demon magic hat."
- Charles Gould

Deros & Teros

Episode 140: The Deros and Teros

Strengths: Telepathy, Pain Rays

Weaknesses: Slow moving, Stupid

Physical Description: Toothless, Gummy mouth, No Nipples, Obese, Long elephant noses

In 1943, Richard Shaver wrote a letter to Amazing Stories where he revealed that he discovered the world of the Deros (stands for Detrimental Robots). There were elevators located in Washington, Chicago and Midtown Manhattan. If you went to the basement in the elevator then proceeded to hit the "B" button twice, the elevator would go down even further and shift to the left. The doors would then open to the world of the Deros. Toothless, pig-like creatures with no nipples who happen to come up every now and then to purchase food.

The Deros killed Richard's brother and then brainwashed him to commit a crime that was too sorted to describe. He then went to prison and the Deros began to shoot rays into his brain which kept him in terrible pain.

One night while in prison, he was visited by a hot sexy blind alien in a dream and he could see her bra with a little green bow. The alien then returned the next day, hypnotized the guard and broke Richard out of prison.

This alien's name was Nidia and she was a member of the underground dwelling monsters called the Teros who fight the disgusting Deros.

Quotes:

"You sick or something?"
- Clocky

"No, I just don't like...welding anymore"
- Richard Shaver

Djinn

Episode 134: The Almighty Djinn

Strengths: Shapeshifter, Ability to possess humans, Scary as heck, Creepy laugh

Weaknesses: Easily tricked, Solomon's ring, Bottles, Unwashed underwear under the pillow, Prayers from an Imam

Physical Description: Devious creatures made of smokeless fire, Summoned from bottles, Voiced by Robin Williams (of Flubber fame)

Djinn are shape-shifting creatures that have been living in this universe since long before the creation of Man, but these aren't your friendly genies from Disney's Aladdin. These genies have been banished to another dimension and will do whatever it takes to reclaim their stake on this world.

The Djinn were created of smokeless fire by Allah and were placed on Earth as stewards but eventually separated into clans that battled each other and destroyed most of the Earth. Allah sent an army of Angels to cast the Djinn into a parallel world, but some were allowed to stay and help repair the world for God's newest creation, Adam. God commanded that all his Angels and Djinn bow to his new creation, but the Djinn refused and were banished to hell for eternity.
God gave the Djinn until judgment day to prove that humans were not worthy of his love and gave them the power to lead humankind astray.

During the construction of King Solomon's temple, a Djinn attacked the son of a beloved master builder and sucked his life force from his right thumb. Solomon was given a ring with the seal of a pentagram from the Archangel Michael that he used to lock up Djinn and force them to build his temple, becoming the original Green Lantern. To protect humanity, Solomon imprisoned many Djinn in brass bottles which is where the legend of magic lamps originates. Djinn have been known to kill many humans including fathers with candy, rickshaw drivers and guys dumb enough to not marry a Djinn when offered. You can't fight a Djinn.

Quotes:
"How Long...25!!!"   "You can't fight a Djinn"   "Bad...huh?....bad"

DOGMEN

Episode 152: The Doglike-Arnold-Monster of Central Pennsylvania
Episode 175: The Michigan/Wisconsin Dogman

Strengths: Jacked like Arnold, Huge claws, Sharp teeth, Eats cats

Weaknesses: People making out, Roadkill, Sequels

Physical Description: It's got a wolf face and head and an animal wolf like body that is very muscular that almost looks like a human that would be working out.

Dogmainia struck in 1987 when a Michigan DJ released a song titled "The Legend" based on actual reports of a dog-like cryptid. "The Legend" became the most requested song on WTCM that year and was so popular that two years later Steve Cook would write a sequel that was NOT POPULAR. In 1997, ten years after the release of the original, Cook released a newer/hipper version of the song called "The Legend '97".

Since then there have been many reports of the elusive Dogman including a witness who took a picture of the creature peeking out from behind a pole and multiple reports of the Dogman peeking into cars when teenagers were making out. One report claimed that he looked like a man in a gorilla outfit and smelled like shit.

The Dogman was featured on the History Channel show Dog Quest where a Michael Winslow type was quoted as saying "WRORRRRRER! Holy cow that was no buck in rut!" and "Shewewewoww. Whomp! That thing just jumped out of a tree!". The episode also featured Dr. Lynn Rodgers who analyzed hair samples that were determined to be nothing but a plain old cat.

The Pennsylvania Dogman was featured on Coast to Coast AM and was described as a giant dog that was jacked up like Arnold Schwarzenegger. One caller claimed the Dogman ate his cat and that he saw it riding the bus. It has also been claimed that the Dogman is a Native American spirit which was described in depth by Unbeliever Judy in an on-air interview.

Quotes:

"I seen this animal riding the bus when I crossed in front of the bus, I got off of the bus."

"I'm really good at it!"

"I think it ate my cat."

DOLPHINS

Mentioned on many episodes mostly along the lines of "we should do an episode on Dolphins"

Strengths: Psychic, Telepathy, Teleportation, Electroreception

Weaknesses: Mammal problems, Rapey

Physical Description: 5 to 30 foot long aquatic mammals with streamlined bodies and two limbs that are modified into flippers.

The Dolphins work with Carol Croft to distribute Orgonite throughout the world's oceans, accumulating them near secret government bases. Millions of years of evolution relying on complex communication has given them the ability to both decipher and converse in nearly every human and alien language. They are a longtime ally of humans. Dolphins are a gift to us from the Pleiadians and are here to heal us.

They can leave anytime they want to like in the Douglas Adams books and are 5th dimensional or whatever.

Dolphins do not need to sleep. They have a visual range of 300 degrees, and can operate each eye independently allowing them to see in two directions simultaneously. They can see in the exceptionally low light, both in and out of the water. They can hear frequencies up to 10 times the upper limit of humans and have supernatural healing and regeneration. Their antimicrobial skin is twenty times thicker than ours. They are incredibly strong and efficient at turning calories into thrust. They can turn off pain and have magnetite crystals in their brain that help them sense magnetic fields for accurate navigation in the featureless void of the ocean.

Sonar allows them to know the location, size and shape of objects and creatures within hundreds of feet of them. They use electroreception to sense the electrical impulses given off by all living things.

Did You Know:

Brian Frange wore a Dolphins "Starter" jacket in middle school because he liked the color teal.

DUMBEST ALIENS

Episode 164: The Dumbest Alien Stories Ever
Volume 1

Strengths: Viagra gel, Smarter than hicks, Space travel

Weaknesses: Fertilizer, Need for water, Incoherent jabbering

The Fertilizer Aliens who are four feet tall, speak perfect English, are from Mars and took a 75-pound bag of fertilizer from Gary Wilcox to terraform their planet.

The Giant Space Brains of Palos Verdes are bluish in color and have a red eye in their frontal lobe. They told John Hodges, "Take the time to understand yourselves, the times draw near when you shall need to. You shall not remember this incident until we meet again. Brainnnsss!".

The Pascagoula Wrinkly Elephant aliens came in a football-shaped craft and had two stumps that appeared to be melded together for legs, no eyes, small slit for a mouth, three carrot-like appendages protruded from the face where the nose and ears would be, and large lobster claws for hands.

The Viagra Gel Aliens abducted Antonio Vilas Boas in a purple UFO. They stripped him naked and sprayed a strange liquid over his body which made him super horny. A sexy female alien, that growled like a dog, had sex with him then pointed to her belly and up to the sky.

The Drunken Indians is a story about two aliens that stole a car from two drunken Native Americans and "jabbered incoherently like a woman or a bird". Then they left.

The Italians were three aliens that landed in Joe Simonton's yard and had an empty jug. Joe filled the jug with water and the Italians saluted him. One of the Italians was making pancakes that tasted like cardboard and were extremely greasy. The Italians then flew away. Joe sent the remaining pancakes to the airforce for investigation. It was determined that they were pure buckwheat pancakes.

Quotes:

"They were pure buckwheat pancakes"

"Jabbered incoherently like a woman or a bird"

"Brainnsss!"

FREDDY ALIENS

Episode 153: Alien in the Freezer

Strengths: Dog killer, Contact causes illness and pants filling, Voice sounds like tape and can cause headaches

Weaknesses: Freezers, Men in Black, Tree branches

Physical Description: Four foot tall childlike alien creatures with mature features wearing black jumpsuits.

In 1996, Jonathan Reed's golden retriever Suzy was attacked and killed by a four-foot tall childlike creature while on a walk in the woods. Reed found Suzy engaged in "mortal com...conflict" and struck the being on the head with a tree branch, apparently killing the attacker. Reed immediately became sick to his stomach and began throwing up and filling his pants.

Reed brought the alien home and put him in the freezer. His friend Gary concluded that the alien looked like his boss Freddy, so they named it Freddy. After a few days, Reed heard a strange noise emanating from the freezer. He looked inside and, to his surprise, saw that Freddy was still alive. Freddy began communicating with Reed through a shrill chirping sound that sounded like tape being pulled. He recorded audio of this chirping and during the recording complained like a bitch that the sound hurt his head.

After 9 days of living with Freddy, Jonathan came home to a ransacked house and both Freddy and the freezer were gone. He saw little-frozen footprints that stopped at the wall. He believes the Men in Black are responsible for destroying his home but does not believe they captured Freddy. Reed believes that Freddy stays near him like a shadow and says the creature is "in the hands of his own".

Quotes:

"Be throwing up and filling my pants" - Jonathan Reed

"He's in the hands of his own" - Jonathan Reed

"Mortal Kom...conflict" - Jonathan Reed

GLOWING ORBS

Episode 215: Can You Trust Stan Romanek Part 1
Episode 222: Skinwalker Ranch Part 1

Strengths: Flight, Can pass through solid objects, Possibly ghosts or aliens, Kill dogs

Weaknesses: Non aggressive, Possibly just dust or lens flare

Physical Description: Glowing balls of light associated with ghost and alien experiences.

Glowing orbs sometimes referred to as "Ghost Orbs" or "Spirit Orbs", are a paranormal phenomenon associated with alien and ghost experiences. Rarely seen with the naked eye, Glowing Orbs are commonly seen in photographs and videos taken during paranormal events or in cemeteries.

Alleged alien contactee Stan Romanek has taken multiple videos of these orbs and claims they are related to his alien experiences. The Glowing Orbs have also been sighted at Skinwalker Ranch where they are referred to as the "Blue Meanies". Skinwalker Ranch resident Tom Gorman claims that he sighted these orbs while sitting on the back porch with his 3 big hunting dogs. The dogs were drawn to the objects and began barking wildly and snapping at them. The "Blue Meanies" led his dogs far from his house and out of sight. Later, Tom heard three horrible shrieks and the next day found 3 greasy spots on the ground. This was all that was left of his dogs after their encounter with the orbs.

Another notable experience with orbs comes from Unbeliever Jude. While taking pictures of his impressively wide windows for his interior designer girlfriend, Jude spotted a strange entity in the corner of his camera. The entity glowed radiantly and had the shape of a humanoid. He tried to take more photos of the being, but it ran straight across the room and disappeared. His remarkable photos have yet to be explained!

Quotes:

"I'm sick of fucking orbs"
   - Brian Frange

"I bet you if I look long enough,
I can find an orb" - Brian Frange

"I'd like to see you make a video
of an orb" - Phoebe Tyers

ILLUMINATI

Members: Queen Elizabeth, Henry Kissinger, The Pope, Madonna (Drake?), Jay Z, Alex Jones, Bill Clinton, Arianna Grande's Mom, Demi Lovato, Putin

Episode 114: Fritz Springmeier's 13 Bloodlines of the Illuminati

Strengths: Money, Robots, Underground bunkers, More than 31 flavors of religion

Weaknesses: Just humans, Mostly old, Multiple-personality disorder

Physical Description: Old white dudes and their celebrity friends

The Illuminati is a secret underground organization that controls the global economy and world politics dating back to the 18th century. Many famous politicians and celebrities are believed to be a part of this mysterious group.

Christian Conservative researcher Fritz Springmeier dedicated his life to exposing the 13 Illuminati Bloodlines that have been running the world for Centuries. That is until he was imprisoned for robbing a bank with an assault rifle.

Their dirty deeds and bloodlines detailed in Springmeier's many books, the Illuminati consists of the rich and powerful who receive their orders from Satan himself.

Quotes:
> "And my apologies to Baskin Robbins, there's more than 31 flavors there."
> - Fritz Springmeier

Immortal Jellyfish

Episode 198: Sea Monsters Part 3 –
Immortal Jellyfish

Strengths: Poison sting, Tons of friends,
Never having to deal with turning 40,
Immortality

Weaknesses: Made of jelly, Stuck in the
water

Physical Description: Gooey, Tentacled,
Immortal, No bones, Kind of look like
spaceships

Though we may not be able to see them from satellite, the jellyfish are almost
certainly destined to rule the oceans of Earth. Even growing legs with which to
climb upon the land and rule the surface world as well (well, probably not.) If that
isn't bad enough, some of them are apparently immortal...

In 1988, a snorkeling marine biology student repeatedly attempted to murder a
specimen of the jellyfish 'turritopsis dohrnii,' but to no avail! It appeared to age in
reverse, growing younger and younger until it reached its earliest stage of
development to begin its life cycle anew, and achieving potential immortality.
Henceforth it would forever be known as The Immortal Jellyfish.

Quotes:

"We cannot see the jellyfish from
satellite." - Ferdinando Boero

"Mmmm, mm, mmm"
- Interviewer

Indigo Children

Ep. 128 The Montauk Chair

Strengths: Telekinesis, Telepathy, Being really smart, Can fly through windows to go to Princeton

Weaknesses: Guns, Growing up, Standardized testing, ADHD, Princeton

Physical Description: They are ordinary children except they have indigo-colored auras and may be bending spoons and levitating.

Not to be confused with the Indigo Girls, Indigo Children arrive on this planet with way more intelligence, creativity and abilities than the Indigo Girls combined. They slowly lose their power as they get older because they get farther and farther away from the center of energy of the universe.

The Indigo Children are here to bring us closer to our essence, and yet Brian is not interested in them at all because he thinks they are spoiled brats with ADHD. He hates that they are born special and should be revered, and despises their superior intelligence. This may stem from jealousy and personal feelings of inadequacy. It could also be because they maintain their own sense of authority, but why should they be expected to listen to their parents and teachers when standardized testing and the public education system makes them unlearn everything they know?

The indigo children are generally accepted to be human children gifted with an "indigo" colored aura (whatever that means) who are prone to ADHD. They are in tune with their inner knowing, according to professional bullshitter Doreen Virtue, whereas the rest of us idiots have supposedly forgotten our ability to tap into the collective consciousness. New Age apologist Nancy Ann Tappe believes that 80% of children born in 1980 and on have this indigo aura, so Brian probably was an indigo child but grew up and forgot his inner knowing, and has at some point replaced his indigo aura with entrepreneur fundraising platform Indiegogo.

Quotes:

"They're not telepathic, they are just uptight annoying little brats and they deserve to be thrown in a cage"

"This sounds like unmedicated kids with ADHD"

Insectoids & Mantis Aliens

Episode 94: The Alien Abduction Phenomena
Episode 241-243: The Man Who Fucks Aliens

Strengths: Original content creators, Mutilating cow anuses, Weaving color and sound to create the light web of the universe. Known as the Universe's vagina.

Weaknesses: Insect repellent, Anti-voyeurism legislation, Premature ejaculation.

Physical Description: Giant insect-like beings, resembling praying mantises. Triangular heads, Very very thin body, very very thin arms and fingers. They typically wear long robes with colors signifying rank.

Popularized by Dr. David Michael Jacobs via the hundreds of abductees he spoke with, the Insectoids are a force to be reckoned with. They are incredibly efficient, well-organized leaders, and are stronger than the Alpha Draconian Reptilians. They may have created the other alien species for use as slaves and have no problem mutilating cow anuses. Most say they are malevolent, but some think they weave color and sound to create the light web of the universe. Most others say no, they're not; they're bad, they're the worst and they are also hideous.

They abduct humans to sexually experiment on but typically use the greys and reptilians to do their dirty work. They are regarded as the founders and ever-wise controllers of the universe, which is confusing because they are also a bunch of cuckolded chumps. Popular theory states that their propensity toward premature ejaculation led them to create the greys to have sex with humans in their place while they're relegated to watching in the corner, but it could be that they just know what gets them off and everyone else has no choice but to be their sex slaves.

They are frequently referred to as the universe's vagina, and we may very well be fragments of that collective consciousness. Nobody really likes that idea though, because it begs the question of what the universe's dick might be, and whether or not this means that the universe fucked itself.

Quotes:
"The mantis aliens can't help but prematurely ejaculate when they see David, so they created this being that could have sex with David while they watch."

"You don't wanna get fucked by that praying mantis, either, because you know praying mantises, after they fuck they bite off your head."

J. C. Webster III

And Edna P. Pringle, Blade & a big pile of porn

Episode 244-246: Art Bell Tribute Month

Strengths: Fighting demons and pornography, Spitting venom, Living life on the road off-the-grid, Brining new revelations

Weaknesses: Art Bell, Cats, Lack of self-control, Rock n' roll music

God's own 10-Star, 10-Star, 10-Star General in the war against media pornography, JC Webster III spread word of The New Revelation by calling into Coast to Coast AM.

JC Webster III is the leader of CLAMP (Christian Legion Against Media Pornography). His disciple Edna P. Pringle lived on the CLAMP compound with JC where they diligently battled Russians, Canadians, Bigfoot, people who steal toilet paper from supermarket bathrooms, the devil, homosexuals, and all other forms of pornography.

Edna would harass Art Bell with vicious emails defending JC and vilifying Art before she started listening to The Pointer Sisters. Once Edna was exposed to rock'n'roll music and other pornography, she quickly left JC and CLAMP to live a life filled with marijuana cigarettes, menage a trois, and multiple organisms. Prior to her capture and re-brainwashing, she was last seen by JC on the back of Blade's motorcycle, giving him an obscene hand gesture as the two rode off into the sunset with $10,000 of "The Lord's Money".

Blade is a biker. What kind of name is Blade? Who would name their child Blade? A corrupted person. Nothing is known about Blade's upbringing, but he was eager to help Edna blow the stolen $10,000 on fatty foods, candy, gambling, and rock'n'roll music. Blade is a sex machine.

Quotes:

"HOW DAAAREEEE YOOOOU!"
- J. C. Webster III

"I wish Bigfoot were my dad"
- Art Bell

Jersey Devil

Episode 217: The Jersey Devil

Strengths: Flying, Killing midwives, Breathing fire, Has a killer runway walk

Weaknesses: Clergymen, Driving

Physical Description: Face of a horse, Head of a dog, Kangaroo body with cloven hooves, A long tail and bat wings

A witch in Leeds Point wished that her 13th child would be a devil and was granted her wish on a stormy night in 1735. It flew up the chimney and into the pine barrens immediately after its birth, so she couldn't even show off her devil baby to her coven or anything. Other accounts claim that due to the ungodly pain from childbirth she cried out, "This must be the devil!". Still, one more version says the child was born as a blond cherubic child that then transformed before its mother's eyes and killed the midwife before flying up the chimney. Its shrieks were heard nightly from the swamps for several years until a clergyman put the Jersey Devil to rest for 100 years.

Early on it was described as a gentle imp, but most accounts of the devil are as terrifying as the name suggests. The hoof prints are always single-file and can continue on the other side of an impossibly high wall as though no wall was there. Some have seen it while driving on a rural road, flying and shrieking toward their vehicle with fiery eyes, blowing smoke and flame, with the smell of burning lingering in the air long after the encounter.

The Jersey Devil once crashed its Volkswagen Jetta into the vehicle of the bipolar Stark family, and later had the shit beat out of it by the very pregnant Wendy Stark while her worthless family looked on. Numerous rewards have been offered for its capture dead or alive, but despite the high volume of sightings, no reward has been claimed.

Quotes:

"What a cockamamie."
– Everyone

"Can the Devil not leave New Jersey?" – Kevin Cobbs

"I got my whole family to say 'woo!' I'm the BEST daughter." – Brian Frange

Kentucky Goblins

Episode 158: Kentucky Goblins

Strengths: Back flips, Agility, Made out of metal (maybe?)

Weaknesses: Shotgun Blasts

Physical Description: Tiny, Green, Silver Jumpsuits

One night in August of 1955, a backwoods family known as the Sutton's were terrorized by little green men. Billy Ray went to fetch a pail of water and saw a flying saucer off in the distance. His family didn't believe him at first but eventually got on board with his story.

They quickly boarded up all of the windows and doors, then pulled out a bunch of shotguns. The men of the family stepped outside to see little green men wearing silver jumpsuits. When shooting at the goblins, the men would scream at the top of their lungs. It sounded like their bullets were hitting metal and the goblins would then do a backflip.

Once police arrived, they inspected the bullet hole riddled house and the shaken up hillbillies. They concluded that nothing happened.

One popular theory is that a bunch of monkeys escaped from a nearby traveling circus. Another theory is that they were just a bunch of drunks.

Quotes:

"W. W. Why would I lie about
something like that!"
- Billy Ray Taylor

"If you shoot a monkey, a monkey
is going to fall down and die"

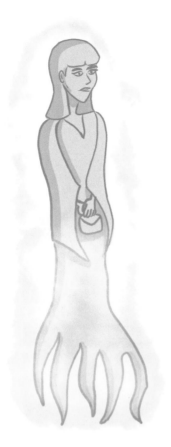

Known Ghosts

Episode 141: Haunted American Cemeteries
Episode 157: Phone Calls From The Dead

Strengths: Prank Calls, Making Out With Dudes

Weaknesses: No weapons or fighting skill

Physical Description: Apparition, Transparent, Spooky

Is there life after death? Ghosts are known to haunt the land of the living after their physical bodies' perish.

Some known ghosts have made contact with the living realm through the use of AM radio. And what do these ghosts have to say? "Hot Dog Art", "This is G", "Merry Christmas and Happy New Year to you all".

In 1959, Konstantin Raudive was able to make contact with deceased Russian poet Vladimir Mayakovsky and what did the ghost say..."Mayakovsky". He was also able to connect with Spanish philosopher Ortega y Gasset who screamed at the top of his lungs "Ortega". Ghosts who are able to connect to the land of the living mostly say their own name similar to a Pokemon.

Another known ghost, Resurrection Mary, is from Justice Illinois. As the legend is told, she was in a horrible hit and run accident a long time ago. Her ghost haunts the Illinois streets hitchhiking at night. Any guy that picks her up, she'll go dancing with and even make out with them. At the end of the night, she has them drop her off at Resurrection Cemetery.

Quotes:

"I don't understand what brought me here."

"Basket of Apples."

"That's the guy's name Phoebe!"

KORENDIANS

Episode 111: The Korendians of Korendor

Strengths: Radio communication. Light. Love.
Brotherhood. Peace. Spiritual Awareness.
Superior intelligence. Superior technology.
Advanced society

Weaknesses: Physical violence

Physical Description: Human in appearance,
about 4' - 5' tall. No eyebrows or hair, smaller
flat ears, small nose with slit nostrils, longer
webbed fingers. Tanned like a Californian.

Korendians are benevolent, humanoid aliens from Korendor in the Bootes
Constellation. They have an advanced society and technology so superior to ours,
we may as well be riding around in chariots. They have a long life span and their
self-appointed role is that of "gardeners of the earth". They help to advance our
race by imprinting their philosophies on us in our sleep and by using their powers
of love, light, peace and spiritual awareness to fight against the Omegans and the
Kalrans, two evil species of aliens who each want control of Earth. Due to their
prime directive, they're not allowed to interfere openly and can only guide us to
make our own decisions, but they also are still down to hook up with electronics
wizards like Bob Renaud.

Bob has transcribed over 50 years of communications. He was first contacted in
July of 1961 by Linn-Erri, an associate from Korendor via his ham radio in his
parents' basement. Bob describes the beautiful women who freely give out their
measurements without being prompted, their 11-story spaceship, their philosophies,
and their planet, which is, naturally, a fancier utopic version of Earth but with
way more oxygen. They are unable to communicate telepathically so they learned
English (with a southern Californian accent) by monitoring our tv shows and
beaming the information into their brains. Their primary goal is disarming our
militaries of nuclear weapons, explaining that they had witnessed the destruction
of entire planets before (like Princess Leia).

Bob was named the Terran Representative and the official spokesman for the
Korendians. His coolness was now off the charts, and a Korendian woman named
Astra-Lari couldn't keep her star lady panties on.

Quotes:

"Are aliens just Californians?"
- Phoebe Tyers

"Jesus was a great space master."
- Brian Frange

KORTON

Known Koldasians: Korton (Cory), Eddie (Oddy), Newt, Um-guy, Janelle, and Instruct Automatic Relay

Episode 207: Alien Contact - This Is Korton

Strengths: Unable to answer questions directly or comprehensively

Weaknesses: Unable to answer questions directly or comprehensively

Physical Description: Unknown

On a show called Weird Weekends, Louis Theroux interviewed Reverend Robert Short and introduced the world to Korton, an extraterrestrial being from Koldas (a planet like our saturn, incidentally these beings used to live in our solar system before a cataclysmic war drove them away).

While fast talking and rolling his R's the Reverend revealed the following. It costs $50 to get the Reverend to channel Korton. Korton is channeled through the back of the nasal cavity and is transmitted through some sort of relay station at Saturn. Korton and his people seem to wish humanity no harm. Channeling causes the good reverend to get very sweaty, so much so that Louis can touch it! Korton would like to convert everyone in the universe to Christianity.

Central Control is a regular workspace that helps individuals get in touch with their favorite Koldasians. During the Reverend's communications, several individuals passed through the office of Central Control, one notable one being Eddy, a nervous Woody Allen type.

George Van Tassel and the Ashtar Command are related to Central Command in that Van Tassel taught Reverend Short how to channel aliens. This may imply a much larger galactic community. During this meeting, Van Tassel used the song "I'm forever blowing bubbles" to contact the aliens. During channeling sessions, Korton takes control of the Reverend's body and vocal cords, and when he comes to he is unaware of anything that happened. Later in the Reverend's life, Korton took on a heavy religious tone and caused him to "wig out" for quite a while as he sits in an oriental shirt and zebra eye mask.

Quotes:

"Animal Sacalorum, is that understood?"
- Reverend Robert Short

"This is Central Control!"
- Reverend Robert Short

"Discontinue, discontinue."
- Reverend Robert Short

Leprechauns & Elementals

Episode 42: Leprechauns
Episode 113: Fairies

Strengths: Lighter than air, Transparent,
Extremely fast, Healing abilities

Weaknesses: Keys, Boiling Egg Shells,
Ovens, Traps

Physical Description: Miniscule beings with
red or green clothing, bearded, often invisible

Leprechauns and Elementals consist of beings such as Gnomes, Elves, Fairies,
Trolls, Giants and traditional Leprechauns. These beings known as "Nature Spirits"
are believed to be descended from angels and have existed long before humanity.
Tales of Leprechauns and Elementals have been a part of Irish and European
folklore for centuries.

The modern experts on Elementals are Christopher Valentine and his lover Dr.
Christian Von Lahr. Valentine had his first experience with these creatures when
he noticed that a book was missing from his shelf, it then reappeared confirming
that a Leprechaun had taken it. His lover Dr. Von Lahr had his first experience
while in a hot tub when an invisible Nature Spirit began throwing his clothes into
the hot tub. These experts claim that Elementals once lived in the natural world
but as humans invaded nature they decided to move into the human realm. These
creatures will try to enter a home by taking the owner's keys and once inside will
help the human inhabitants by cobbling shoes and fixing broken items.

There are numerous ways to stop the Elementals from inhabiting a house such as
putting them in an oven, distracting them with colorful lights, constructing traps
with whiskey or Heineken beer, or most effectively boiling eggshells.

Did You Know:

   According to Unbeliever lore, former cohost Crystal Delahanty is believed to have been
   carried off by Leprechauns.

Leviathans

Members: The Polypus, The Sea Pig, The Priester, Spermaceti, Sea Serpents

Episode 196: Sea Monsters Part 1- The Olaus Magnus Map

Strengths: Massive size, Skins its victims, Poisonous, Can sink ships, Gross

Weaknesses: Farts, Trumpets, Infighting, Mostly confined to water

Physical Description: Varied from 200 feet tall behemoths to puddles of sperm

The Leviathans are a collection of sea monsters from the Olaus Magnus map. Created in 1539, the "Carta Marina" was a map of Scandinavia and its surrounding area created by the Swedish writer and priest Olaus Magnus. The map was the largest and most detailed of the time, including the many monsters that inhabited the surrounding seas.

The team includes the Polypus, a giant color-changing lobster that eats the unfortunate souls it comes across. It removes their skin in its lair and uses the skin as bait to lure other sea creatures. The only defense against the Polypus is foul smells, such as farts, that will repel the beast. Joining the Polypus is the Sea Pig, a 72-foot long sea monster with a hog like head. The Sea Pig has weird red eyes covering its body, scaled fins, four dragon-like feet, a forked fin and poisonous spines. The poison can cause great pain and the only cure is to drink the bile from the Sea Pig's stomach.

The Priester is a towering horse shaped beast with a dragon-like chest and a powerful waterspout that is known to sink ships. As menacing as this monster may be, the Priester cannot endure the sound of a trumpet. If this Leviathan hears a trumpet sounded it will flee in fear.

The classic Sea Serpent is a 200-foot tall behemoth that lives close to the coast of populated areas. The Sea Serpent is over 20 feet thick, has flaming eyes that shine and sharp scales covering its body. The Sea Serpent can also go on land to kill livestock. Sea Serpents are known to devour men from their ships to warn of changes in the kingdom. Last and certainly least is Spermaceti. This is a phenomenon where a vast expanse of whale sperm is floating in the sea.

Quotes:

"I fart constantly dude!"
- Sebastian Conelli

"You can fart in it's face, but what if you don't have one?"- Phoebe Tyers

Little Girl

Episode 222: Skinwalker Ranch - Part One

Strengths: Invisibility, Stealth, Possibly impervious to harm?

Weaknesses: We don't know

Physical Description: No physical form (that we know of)

The Little Girl is the disembodied voice of an adolescent female that whispers softly around Skinwalker Ranch in northeastern Utah. Much is unknown about her, like her origin, what she looks like, what the hell she is whispering about and if she's even speaking English. According to Ryan Skinner, who wrote several books on Skinwalker Ranch, the chances of seeing the Little Girl are unknown.

What is known is that whatever she is saying is so hard to hear, she can't possibly hurt anyone's feelings, which is more than can be said about the invisible shit-talking helicopters found elsewhere on the ranch. She could be talking mad shit too, but what you can't hear very well can't hurt you very well.

The extent of her power has yet to be determined; she might have the ability to sway luck in her favor, or the power of (un)believing in herself. It's uncertain whether she's capable of physically obliterating her opponents, but she did manage to whisper her way to the top of the Skinwalker Ranch Mini Tournament, outlasting the likes of the Sentient Mist, the Blue Meanies and the Bulletproof Wolf. Considering how rare encounters are with the Little Girl, and how little is known about her, it stands to reason that she must have very high stealth stats or even invisibility, which is a useful advantage in the Tournament of Aliens.

Quotes:

"I have never experienced this voice but when she speaks I'm certain she is by herself." - Ryan Skinner

"The little girl is unknown. The possibilities are endless."
- Sebastian Conelli

LIZARDMAN

Episode 142: The Bishopville Lizardman

Strengths: Biting cars, Scaring fast food employees, Inspiring great Washtar music

Weaknesses: No feet, Relentlessly mocked on late night TV, Lives in a swamp named after an escaped whore

Physical Description: 7 foot tall Reptile, Red eyes, No feet, Sharp three-fingered claws

Back in 1988 a half-man, half-lizard began chewing up cars in a swampy old town in South Carolina. Residents dubbed the creature the Lizardman and Lizardmania swept the town. It all started with the report of a 1985 Ford LTD getting "chewed up" in Browntown followed by later reports of a seven-foot tall creature with red eyes living in Scapeor (Escape Whore) Swamp. Things escalated quickly when the Lizardman chased a McDonald's employee who's drawing of the monster (with no feet) sparked Lizardmania in Bishopville.

The Lizardman was covered by Good Morning America, the LA Times, Time magazine and People magazine. Most importantly, the Lizardman became the subject of musician Roy Atkinson who created the greatest song ever written titled "Lizardman Stomp". Roy, who invented an instrument for his severely handicapped son called the Washtar, composed the definitive Lizardman song and changed the course of musical history with his incorporation of a washboard glued to a guitar and lyrics about a mythical Lizardman.

The Lizardman Stomp lives on to this day and has been recently covered by musician Aaron Schlib, breathing new life to a legend that just won't go away. The Lizardman was also the inspiration for the world-renowned children's book "Lizardmania" written by Unbeliever Carey and illustrated by Jawadog. The book teaches tolerance and acceptance to tens of children.

Quotes:

"What's a Newt?"
- Phoebe Tyers

"Sometimes I get my girlfriend to play the old dick-tar"
- Saurin Choksi

LOCH NESS MONSTERS & CHAMPY

Strengths: Excellent swimmer, Elusive, Nice neck

Weaknesses: No real legs, Not photogenic, Introverted

Physical Description: Essentially a plesiosaur,
complete with flippers, a humped back, and a long
neck (good for reaching things on high shelves)

The Loch Ness Monster is a cryptid (possible plesiosaur) that has been haunting
the waters of Loch Ness in Scotland for centuries. One of the first documented
sightings was by Irish Monk St. Columba in 565 AD. Ever since, thousands of
accounts, photographs, and footage have appeared year after year from those
claiming to have seen the elusive beast.

Though we are pretty sure Nessie is real (Scotland agrees), many claim that it
could also be a seal, a Wels catfish, or possibly an odd wave. Adding to the
confusion, many people who have claimed to have spotted Nessie, or captured her
on film, have later admitted that they lied or faked the photo in some way. George
Edwards, a tour boat operator on the loch, went as far as to create a monster out
of fiberglass in order to drum up business.

Among the many that hunt for proof of Nessie, the saddest hunter of them all is
Steve Feltham. Since 1991, Feltham has kept vigil on the banks of the loch with his
trusty van/office/home filled with clay models of Nessie that he sells to fund his
search. One day, he hopes to own a boat and really get down to business.

A distant, Yankee cousin to Nessie, Champy roams the waters of Lake Champlain
on the borders of New York and Vermont. Sandra Mansi took a photograph in 1977
that could be Champy, but is most likely a log. Champ was the inspiration for an
epic song by Stan Ransom and is the mascot of a minor league baseball team.

Quotes:

"Ask Women!"
   - Brian Frange

"Just like the bottom of an upturned boat,
but more humpy."

MARTIANS

Episode 106: The Earth Defense Force and Battling Aliens on Mars
Episode 126: Andrew Basiago and Project Pegasus

Strengths: Stealth, Flash guns

Weaknesses: Fighting ability, Physical strength

Physical Description: Native Martian, Small Grey, Ancient Homosapien, Predator Monsters, Ninja turtle

According to Captain Kaye, native Martian reptilians refer to their planet as Gaa'Lu'Ka and themselves as Gaa'Lu'Kans. They are in a constant battle with humans and insectoids to wipe out the opposing soldiers, but not eradicate them to the point where a vacuum would emerge and invite in a new enemy army.

Basiago describes several different Martians. Native Martians were placed on Mars before a solar catastrophe and have been breeding amongst themselves for 11,500 years. Over one million of them currently live under the surface of Mars. They are homosapien cousins to humans and we can still have sex with them, but they're very pale and have lost most of their hair.

The Greys were left behind by other members of their civilization thousands of years ago. They are very stealthy and can sneak around on roofs without being detected, however, they live underground in a Shire-like environment. Predator Monsters cannot be outrun, outmaneuvered, or stunned by a Flash Gun. They are so terrible, so large, and so vicious that Martian Chrononauts we're given cyanide pills to commit suicide with if they were ever cornered by one. The technology for the Mars Jump Room was given to the United States by grey aliens. The jump room looked like an elevator but would transport the occupants to Mars in about 20 minutes.

In the 1980's, Andy Basiago was a martian Chrononaut with Barry Soetoro, who is more commonly known as former United States President Barack Obama.

Quotes:

"A gray! On the roof! Observing us!"
- Andy Basiago

"What am I going to do without any feet?"
- Andy Basiago

MEL'S HOLE SEAL

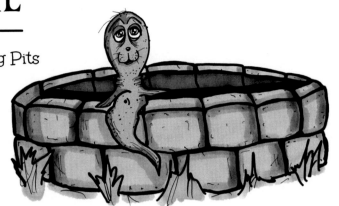

Episode 145: Mel's Hole and Other Gaping Pits

Strengths: Compassionate eyes, Cancer healing, Staring contests

Weaknesses: Sheep guys, Holes

Physical Description: A cross between a fetus and a seal with compassionate human eyes.

In 1995, Mel Waters moved to Manastash in Eastern Washington. On his rural plot of land, he discovered a very big and very deep hole.

Two years later, Mel contacted Coast to Coast AM host Art Bell to tell him about his bottomless hole. Art put Mel in contact with a group of Native Americans who had discovered a second hole and they began conducting experiments, one involving a sheep in a crate.

The sheep began screaming as they attempted to lower it into the hole so the Native Americans punched it until it was unconscious. After dropping the sheep 1500 feet, they brought the sheep back up and found that it was dead. They cut the sheep open and found a large tumor inside. They cut open the tumor and to their shock, a creature emerged that looked like a cross between a fetus and a seal with compassionate human eyes. The seal sat on the ledge and stared at them for two hours, then crawled to the edge of the hole and jumped in. After this incident, Mel discovered that his cancer had been healed. The seal creature was never to be seen again.

Quotes:

"Uh yeah..about that hole?"
- Coast 2 Coast AM Caller

"I'm no sheep guy but i can pick up a sheep." - Mel Waters

Men in Black

Episode 110: The Real Men in Black + Illuminati Oscars

Strengths: Telepathy, Teleportation, Dirty looks, Mind erasing

Weaknesses: The Neighbors

Physical Description: Dark suits, Sunglasses

The Men in Black are a mysterious group of men in black suits that appear after UFO sightings and intimidate witnesses into silence. Dressed all in black, they have shrill sounding voices and only appear human from a distance. They sometimes have cables and hoses coming out of their shoes. Accounts of the Men in Black began during the "Saucer Craze" of the 1950's when famed Ufologist Albert K. Bender claimed that a group of men in black suits had threatened him and warned him to stop his investigation of flying saucers.

Another notable account of the Men in Black is from John Keel, author of the "Mothman Prophecies". During the Mothman sightings of 1966/1967, the Men in Black were sighted many times by people who claimed to witness the creature. Keel described them as having dark skin and "exotic" facial features, he also believed that they were demonic supernatural beings or Laplanders.

The Men in Black are particularly interested in individuals who have information about alien bases. Their goal was to get witnesses to forget what they have seen. According to alien contactee Victor Zordov, the Men in Black are highly developed robots. They possess a great intellect, are clairvoyant, can teleport and a single look from hem can cause great pain and memory loss. The only known way to stop them is if the neighbors appear, they fear neighbors and will leave if spotted by them.

Are the Men in Black a secret government organization? Are they robots? Are they aliens or demonic creatures? We don't know.

Did You Know:

The movie "Men In Black" is still the highest-grossing action buddy comedy of all time.

Mermaids

Episode 87

Strengths: Fast swimmers, Underwater breathing, Singing can lure men to their doom, Probably sexy

Weaknesses: Land, Sea witches

Physical Description: Half-human, half-fish. Orientation of halves is up for debate.

Mermaids have existed for centuries and first appear in legends dating back to the ancient Greeks and Assyrians, but possibly could have existed earlier. The most popular tale of mermaids is from The Little Mermaid, which was written by Hans Christian Anderson in 1836 and was later made into a Disney movie.

Mermaids (and mermen) are an aquatic-based half human, half fish and are found around the world. Popular culture has adopted the human-on-top, fish-on-bottom version, out of fear of the alternative. There is also a chance that the opposite orientation of fish and human parts may exist. Both versions are possible, though their general existence is often disputed.

In general, both in art and legend, mermaids are depicted to be pleasing to the eye. There are outliers -- some depictions are quite the opposite, ranging from tiny, disfigured mostly-fish creatures, to demonic sea-wretches.

Though there have been many sightings and hoaxes throughout the span of centuries, there has not been any verifiable proof that mermaids exist, according to the NOAA. Most often, sightings are actually just mistaken identity cases of manatees or other large fish. There are currently a select few people that are paid to be mermaids in casino fish tanks. There is also a slew of disenchanted housewives that have shirts asserting that they are, in fact, mermaids. The jury is still out on that.

Did You Know:

Charles once fell in love with a mermaid.

MK ULTRA SUPER SOLDIERS

Episode 107: The Story of MK Ultra Survivor John Stormm

Strengths: Picking up cars and flipping them over, Punch through walls and jump out of buildings, Martial Arts, Dense muscles and bones, Mind control, Remote Viewing

Weaknesses: Controlled by Illuminati, Erased memory, Follow orders

Physical Description: Human men and women of varied size, Top physical condition, Ponytails

MK Ultra is a secret CIA mind control program that experimented on human subjects to develop mind control techniques that would be used against the Communist threat. This project created super soldiers, the perfect mind controlled killing machine.

John Stormm was adopted as an infant by Nazi doctors from Project Paperclip who inducted him as an MK Ultra subject. He was told that his father was killed by Communists in the Korean war and that he was being trained to kill them for his country. Though most failed, John was a success story and was able to survive the rigorous training and body altering to become a killing machine for the government. John's bones were strengthened by a process called Microfracturing and his muscles strengthened by electroshock pads.

By age 17 he was being used in countless secret missions to battle communists and drug cartels. He could pick up your car and flip it over, jump off a fourth-floor building and hit the ground running, take the head on impact of a vehicle going 40 mph without injury and punch at an average speed of 4 times per second with a force of 1600 lbs per square inch.

Ultras are trained in remote viewing and astral projection. They are the product of government manipulation and can be called into action without any control of their own. It is believed that the entire MK project was founded and controlled by the Illuminati.

Quotes:

"I can pick up your car and flip it over!"
- John Stormm

MOTHMAN

Episode 129: The Mothman.
Episode 214: The Mothman Returns.
Episode 223: Mothman Festival 2017

Strengths: Harbinger of death, Disrupting make out sessions, Flight, Can reach speeds of 100 mph

Weaknesses: Laplanders/Orientals, Menstruation, John Keel, 2 questions

Physical Description: 8 foot tall, Glowing red eyes (checking you out), Bird like appearance, Huge wingspan, Muscular build

The strange bird-like humanoid was first spotted in 1966 in Point Pleasant, WV. The first sighting was by five gravediggers. Days later, two young couples saw the creature when "driving" in a remote area. The glowing red eyes approached their car and took the form of an eight-foot-tall winged monster. The teens sped away at 100 mph, but the creature followed and kept pace. The 3rd sighting was the next day when a couple was driving in the same area and spotted the creature and a UFO in the sky. One woman who sighted the Mothman became frozen with fear and fell on her baby. She assumed the baby was dead, but it was fine.

The Men in Black mysteriously appeared in town and tried to drink Jell-O. Locals reported having strange visions of presents floating in the river and weird numbers. The sightings came to a head on the night of December 15, 1966 when the Silver Bridge collapsed, killing 46 people. The Mothman was sighted at the bridge prior to the disaster which has led some to believe that the entity is a demonic creature that warns of calamitous events.

Investigator John Keel linked the Mothman with blood and asked women if they were on their menstrual cycle. He found animals that had their anus's removed because we know that radioactivity settles in the anus. The sightings of the Mothman temporarily stopped after the bridge collapse. Since then it has been spotted in New Orleans, Lacrosse, and most recently in Chicago.

Point Pleasant is now famous for the Mothman and hosts an annual festival with a Mothman museum, a Mothman beauty contest (where you must answer 2 questions) and an impressive statue of the creature. The festival has been attended by both Phoebe and Brian as well as many dedicated Unbelievers.

Quotes:

"We know that radioactivity settles in the anus" - John Keel

"It was disgusting" - Kimmy Beep Bop

THE ORANGE

Strengths: Unknown

Weaknesses: Unknown

Physical Description: They are orange aliens.

Not much is known about The Orange.

Did You Know:

No one really knows much about The Orange. Do you?

Paranormal Video Games

Episode 146: Video Game Strangeness

Strengths: Cause heart attacks, Suicide and seizure inducing, Can kill love life, Creepy music

Weaknesses: Require electricity, Created by humans, Can be defeated by cheat codes

Physical Description: Varied from tall Arcade games to home consoles and handheld devices

Video games have been a major part of many millennials lives but some games are weird and fucked up and kill you.

The most deadly member is the 1980's arcade classic Berzerk. Berzerk was designed by Allen McNeal based on a dream he had about fighting robots in a hallway. In the game, the player would have to shoot robots to advance and avoid the smiley faced villain Evil Otto. One year after the game's release, a young man named Jeff Daley placed in the top ten with a high score of 16660 and dropped dead of a heart attack. A year later another man, 18 year-old Peter Bukowski, dropped dead in a similar fashion after posting in the top ten twice in a fifteen minute period.

The original Pokemon game for the Nintendo Gameboy featured a location called Lavender Town which held a Pokemon graveyard and played very creepy music. The music contained high pitched notes that only children could hear. These notes would cause headaches and lead some Japanese children to commit suicide.

Sonic CD featured bonus levels accessed by secret codes. When entering a secret code, the game would play without warning the sound of a Djinn laughing and an image of a demon Sonic with Mario's face. Japanese text would also appear with the message "Fun is Infinite" and the word "Djinn".

Quotes:

"I gave their culture...honor"
- Brian Frange

"Fun is Infinite"
- Haunted Sega Game

"I'll back pocket that joke for when I see a kid hanging" - Sebastia Conelli

Phil Schneider's Dick

Episode 31
Episode 121: Phil Schneider Revisited

Strengths: Tiny, Mobile, Spits sticky liquid

Weaknesses: Tiny, Soft, Harmless

Physical Description: Oddly similar to the Space Slug from the Star Wars universe however this beast is only the size of a single digit.

It's quite possible that being split in two, like a hot dog, by an alien beam weapon is what gave Phil Schneider's mangled member it's amazing powers, what with the driving and all.

It started on a crisp autumn day in 1979 when a young Philip Schneider, a structural engineer for the US government, found himself descending below the arid landscape of Dulce, New Mexico. As the lift clattered to a stop at the bottom of the immense hole he was confronted by several grey beings of unknown origin. A battle ensued, smoky blue light and the crack of firearms filled the air. Several brave marines laid down their lives to allow Phil to escape, unfortunately, he was no longer a whole man.

You see one of those smoky blue lights has intersected Philips manhood, splitting it in twain like a carnival hotdog.

Unknown to Phil, this series of events had bestowed amazing powers on his dong; for now, it was able to detach, drive a tiny red car, and multiply like so many Mogwai splashed with water.

Quotes:

"Well it crispy crittered my left foot." – Phil Schneider

Pleiadians

Strengths: Space travel, Linguistics, Science and engineering, Long lifespan (~1,000 years)

Weaknesses: Preoccupied with planet Earth

Physical Description: Typically tall, sexy, blonde humanoids. They do not have much excess fat although females are known to have curvy figures.

Pleiadians come from the Pleiades System, a cluster of stars within the constellation Taurus. They are highly evolved humanoids. The Pleiadian realm is the next step in human evolution.

Some of us might be Pleiadians and not even realize it.

We don't know why Pleiadians like us, but they are highly concerned about the planet Earth, it's inhabitants, and how humans could potentially affect the rest of the universe. Pleiadians brought dolphins to Earth. Pleiadians and Reptilians are mortal enemies. They are possibly the ancestors of Native Americans and their Star People.

Although in physical time, the Pleiadians are 541 light years away, they have learned to navigate other worlds, although not always in spaceships. They understand our fear of the unknown, and so they come to help in ways that are non-threatening. They are coming now, sometimes in physical form where they can blend in, but most often through human consciousness. Their intent is not to harm but to help us evolve and develop.

Quotes:

"I had an erection for like 6 hours afterwards and it was pretty painful"

Plejarens

Members: Sfath, Semjase, Ptaah, Nera

Episode 132: The Plejarens Exposed!

Strengths: Time Travel, Lazer guns, Beam ships

Weaknesses: Exclusively make contact with Billy Meier

Physical Description: Nordics; tall, sexy, blonde/light brunette aliens that turn everyone on and have a distinct 60's vibe

The Plejarens are vegetarians from the planet Erra. Their spacecraft (called beamships) look like garbage glued to trash can lids. Like many other aliens of the time, they wish for the people of Earth to stop all forms of war, acts of aggression, crime, hate, discord, bondage, vengeance, and retaliation. They want a form of planetary population control and resource distribution so that the environment is not overtaxed yet can provide resources for everyone.

In 1942 they began contact with Billy Meier. They gave Meier permission to photograph, film, and record their beamships so that he could produce evidence of extraterrestrial visitation.

One time they damaged a tree by flying a beamship too close to it, so they transported the tree back in time to a location where it could effectively recover. Meier initially called these being Pleiadians but later discovered that they do not come from the constellation Pleiades but from another space-time configuration in another dimension 80 light years beyond the Pleiades.

Quotes:

"Unfortunately, almost no one has accepted this apple story of mine."
- Billy Meier

Prism of Lyra, Sirians & Arcturians

Episode 108: The Prism of Lyra

Strengths: Beginning of humanoid consciousness. Non-physical, Telepathy

Weaknesses: Generally peaceful, Confusing

Physical Description: Non-physical beings made of light and consciousness they can take on many forms. Some are red haired giants. The feline Lyrans are Thundercats.

Lyssa Royal channeled Sasha and Malia who described the history of the Prism of Lyra. One day The Founders wondered what it would be like to fragment and temporally forget integrated existence, so it sent energy through the Prism of Lyra and consciousness separated into 7 different densities. Living beings must navigate these densities to return to the whole.

1st Density - A human fetus
2nd Density - Plants
3rd Density - Humans
4th Density - Dolphins
5th Density - Wisdom and desire to help those in lower densities
6th Density - Buddha or Christ density (Home of the Arcturians)
7th Density - Total Oneness

When The Founders decide to become physical, material beings they look like tall, slender, graceful beings with inquisitive eyes. Arcturians are non-physical beings who can take on the form of whatever belief system an entity they want to interact withholds. Some people see them as angels, some see them as aliens, and some see them as their future selves. The goal of Arcturians is to assist in healing personal and planetary consciousness. They can exchange souls with people who enter Arcturus. All people who are born on Earth pass through Arcturus where they are healed and cared for before being incarnated in the 3rd density.

The first humanoids were Lyrans. They are very positive people who spread love. Lyrans are a feline race of aliens that some (Jawadog) think are Thundercats.

Quotes:

"Nothing heals, nurtures, and rejuvenates the human spirit as completely as the Arcturus Vibration."

Psychics & Channelers

Members: Ivan Teller, The Psychic Twins, The Parrot and Julie Tyers

Episode 161: Channelling Celebrities
Episode 173: Ghost Busting With Phoebe's Mom
Episode 186: The Psychic Twins
Episode 221: The Psychic Parrot

Strengths: Communication with the dead and alien races, Being Phoebe's mom, Gangster rap

Weaknesses: No sense of humor

Many have come and gone that claim to be able to communicate with far-off realms; death, deep space, and the future, but few hold such sway over those domains as the Psychics/Channelers.

Ivan Teller: Medium to the stars (as in dead famous people, not other planets or currently living famous people). Ivan famously channeled Robin Williams in what would later go onto be called his least funny part after Flubber. He plans on writing a posthumous book with Mr. Williams called: I Won't Be Doing That Again! His new side hustle is Psychic Porn, a truly underutilized industry.

The Psychic Twins: Terry and Linda predict future events that typically never come to pass and some that mysteriously do but somehow miss the mark. For instance, they've seen great success for themselves in the TOA. They're also known for their unscripted comedy, and famous SNL appearance where they performed "Yakety yak".

The Parrot: Santos was discovered by Unbeliever Mr. Seekme. This foul-mouthed bird has the power to know that when something leaves the room it still exists, is infinitely smarter than a human child, and can rap like Snoop. Perhaps his greatest strength comes with his overwhelming street cred and ability to talk the talk and walk the walk.

Julie Tyers: The ghost hunting, poltergeist ass-kicking, mom to the one and only Phoebe Tyers. Julie has extensive skills with crystals, spells, and strong words, she will be a formattable opponent in this otherwise no star team.

Quotes:

"You fucked up a beak, and now I'm a freak." - Santos the Parrot

"Stay away from those...Vic...Victoria Secret models." - Robin Williams

SHADOW PEOPLE

Episode 137: LIVE! Definitive Preview of the Tournament of Aliens, Part I
Episode 220: Shadow People Stories

Strengths: Great at hide-and-seek. Can induce sleep paralysis and intense feelings of dread. Ability to climb and pass through walls and unopened doors. Scare the shit out of people

Weaknesses: Jesus. Day time and rooms with lights on. Hugs

Physical Description: Shadowy forms accompanied by a feeling of dread that appear in shadows and corners wearing wearing an old fashioned hats

Evidenced throughout folklore and works of art of the past, Shadow People (Shadow Person, in singular form) have been haunting humans since the beginning of time. These creatures enjoy scaring the shit out of people, and that's about all that is known of their motives.

People typically encounter them while also experiencing sleep paralysis. They have also been seen fluttering in the peripheral vision of those abruptly awakened. They've reportedly been seen clawing the backs of stomach-sleeping significant others. They are closely related to the Shadow Dogs reported plaguing a fellow Unbeliever.

They are possibly a physical manifestation of unconscious humans stress. They could also originate from an alternate shadow realm that contains hip locales where they commune, drink fancy black coffee with the occasional puffy cloud of cream in homage to Carly Simon's greatest hit, tipping their fancy old-timey hats at passersby who only acknowledge them with an occasional horse eyed look. An alternate explanation for these creatures has been provided by varying guests on Art Bell's Coast to Coast AM radio show. Most notably among them is Helen Hollis, who believes these creatures to be of alien origin and can only be revoked by invoking the "Name of Jesus".

Quotes:

"They suck." - Phoebe Tyers

SINGING CACTI

Episode 151: The Secret Life Of Plants

Strengths: Reads minds, Knowledge of the Japanese alphabet, Prickly exterior

Weaknesses: Mobility, Strength, Fighting, Feels pain

Physical Description: Small cactus in a pot with electrodes hooked to it

In 1966, detective Cleve Baxter hooked a plant up to a polygraph test, then proceeded to torture and beat the shit out of it. Cleve was never the same after this day.

In 1973, a documentary titled "The Secret Life Of Plants" was released. The whole premise is that plants have a consciousness and when hooked up to electrodes, can communicate, sing and even see the future. The star of the documentary was a cactus whose handler was teaching it the Japanese alphabet.

The woman says shyly to the cactus "Dooooh" and the cactus responds "Doh".

Some plants and cacti can sing really well and sometimes have the pleasure of performing with humans. After performing a rendition of Fields of Gold by Sting, one asshole music teacher said: "I teach a lot of children guitar and none of them are as good as this plant".

Quotes:

"Plants know you're going to jerk off before you know you're going to jerk off." - Phoebe Tyers

"What the fuck is this Phoebe...this is what the episode is about?" - Brian Frange

SKINWALKERS

Episode 222: Skinwalker Ranch Part One
Episode 224: Skinwalker Ranch Part Two

Strengths: Shapeshifting, Disguise, Can run
200 MPH

Weaknesses: Supple neck region

Physical Description: A master mimicker, it is difficult
to differentiate an animal from a being that is a
Skinwalker in its morphed state. They are a
human of Native American origin that has the
ability to disguise themselves as any living
being, most frequently seen in forms of
wolves, foxes, coyotes, owls, eagles, or crows. They also appear as a creature with
that of a "hollowed-out dog body" when not in any other recognizable form.

Originating from the Navajo culture, the legend of the skinwalker begins during
the civil war when a Native American faction sided with white homesteaders in
opposition of the Navajo tribe that resulted in a battle of blood. In retaliation, the
land upon which they battled was put under a curse by the Navajo, giving birth to
the Skinwalker. The aforementioned land has become cleverly named Skinwalker
Ranch. While seemingly a legend, there is some truth to the evils of Skinwalkers of
the Skinwalker Ranch, as to this day, members of the Navajo tribe refuse to go
anywhere near the cursed land.

In order for a fleshly human to become a Skinwalker they must fulfill the
requirement of being heartless, as they are required to sacrifice someone they
allegedly love in order to take on the skin of another being. Upon murdering their
loved ones, the aspiring Skinwalker dresses their human flesh in the corpse of
whatever it is they desire to become. Upon the completion of ceremonial rituals,
this newly found evil capability allows Skinwalkers to take the wings of a bird,
the eyes of a fly, the sting of a bee, and the likeness of any S.O.S, perhaps
selling cursed wands under the likeness of one Joshua P. Warren.

Quotes:

"Skinwalker, Skinwalker, Skinwalker."
- Mike Patton of Faith No More

SOS TEAM

The S.O.S. team is a collection of individuals in the paranormal world.

Richard C. Hoagland
Episode 57: The Shard!

The team is led by Richard C. Hoagland who is best known for championing the "Face of Mars" NASA photo and claims that the moon is an alien base with glass structures such as "The Shard".

Joshua P. Warren
Episode 172: The Wishing Machine

Joshua P. Warren is best known for selling paranormal devices such as The Wishing Machine, the Forces of Nature Wand and many books full of paranormal information. Joshua has made several appearances on Coast to Coast AM talking about his latest items.

Steven Gibbs
Episode 183: Time Travel Part 5 - Steven Gibbs Time Machine

Steven Gibbs is a man who appeared on Art Bell's radio program to explain his homemade time machine called the Hyper Dimensional Resonator (HDR). Gibbs claimed that attaching this device to your head and inserting crystals while stroking a stick plate during a full moon would send a person back in time.

Stan Romanek
Episode 215: Can You Trust Stan Romanek

Stan Romanek is a self-proclaimed most abducted individual of all time who became famous with the release of the documentary "Extraordinary: the Stan Romanek Story". Stan claimed to have alien implants in his body, mysterious injuries from aliens and telepathic communication with grey aliens. He also presented numerous photos and videos.

Did You Know:

Unbeliever Rus called into an episode of Coast 2 Coast AM and talked to Joshua P. Warren live on the air.

John Edmonds
Episode 229: Stardust Ranch Part 1
Episode 230: Stardust Ranch Part 2

John Edmonds is the owner of Stardust Ranch. Edmonds is best known for living on a ranch with a high level of alien activity and paranormal experiences. Employing an array of weapons such as katanas and nunchucks, Edmonds wages a nonstop war against the alien invaders that threaten his property.

Quotes:

"Watch out for Richard Hoagland!"

"It's when your fingers stick, while your stroking it."

"Yeah but my mother said I was full of beans so..."

"You can take a couple of sticks or whatever."

"You turn this nob with one hand, while you stroke the stick plate with the other and when you feel that stick you leave the nob in the position..it was in."

"I have no idea where the Hell that come from."

"I don't believe what I just frickin' saw"

"Wowww, now this makes sense!"

SLENDERMAN

Episode 79: Police Drones, Malaysia Flight Update

Strengths: Influence over prepubescent girls from wisconsin, Surrounded by an army of children, Not afraid to be seen

Weaknesses: Prefers to only kill children, May just exist in the realm of Photoshop

Physical Description: Male in appearance, with extremely slender arms and legs and 4 to 8 foot long tentacles protruding from his back and hands that may be used to stride like Dr. Octopus. Stretchable limbs. Typically seen wearing a distinguishable black suit and fedora style hat and a red or grey necktie. Face appears pale and ghostly, as if wrapped in gauze cloth. Long dress shoes. Coat tails.

A supposed fictional creature created by the mind of Eric Knudsen in 2009 for a Photoshop contest for Something Awful. Slenderman has taken on a life of his own in the minds and hearts of children across the globe, but not without the help of the website Creepypasta, a prepubescent favorite. The minds of children have given the idea of this slender-limbed Jack Skellington wannabe a supposed existence in the physical realm.

A notable case of this occurred when two girls in Waukesha, Wisconsin had been in alleged conversation with Slenderman. They had been seeking to climb the ranks of his realm and become his proxies, and in doing so, were given the mission to kill another fellow prepubescent. They managed to lure another 12 year-old girl into the woods, whom they stabbed 19 times in the name of Slenderman. In the physical realm, Slenderman has reportedly been seen in company with his four accomplices: Hoody, Masky, the Rake, and the Observer. He has not yet been seen peering through windows of Stan Romanek's house, however.

Did You Know:

The supernatural creature Slenderman first appeared in a story on the website Creepy Pasta in 2009.

Space Robots

Episode 174 Dumbest Alien Stories Ever
Vol. 2: Dumb Fights Edition

Strengths: Vaping/Smoking hookah sleeping gas, Impervious to arrows

Weaknesses: Climbing trees, Fire, Coins

Physical Description: Looks like a 6' tall walking suit of armor with fiery, goggle-like eyes and a hinged jaw. Kind of looks like Iron Giant.

On September 4th, 1964, 28 year-old Donald Shrum was out bow hunting with some friends in Cisco Grove, CA and soon became separated from his party. He decided to spend that night up in a tree for safety. Donald was soon visited by two short humanoid aliens and their space robot, and they were not good at climbing trees.

The robot was all about that vape life and would emit a type of toxic smoke from his metal jaw that made Donald go to bed within seconds. During the moments that he was passed out, the Too Short aliens would attempt to climb the tree until he awoke shortly after, causing them to retreat and send the robot back in. This cycle of Donald passing out from bad hookah and almost immediately waking back up repeated for hours.

Donald set fire to his personal items and threw them at the aliens. When he ran out of flammable items, he resorted to throwing his Coinstar coins at them, which they were very fascinated and distracted by.

Eventually, Donald runs out of coins and Too Short finally sends in a 2nd robot. With the robots' combined hookah smoke, Donald this time passes out until morning. He wakes up alone and then proceeds to find his friends and go home.

Quotes:
"The aliens Shrum encountered in the forest might have been a group of Japanese. During WW2, we had trouble with the Japanese." - The U.S. Air Force

"Are you sure this isn't just a Vaudeville routine that someone documented?"
- Sebastian Conelli

Star People

Episode 105: American Indian Aliens - The Stories of Star People

Strengths: Space flight, Telepathy, Advanced civilization, Steal dogs, Can appear and disappear

Weaknesses: Can make mistakes, Can't talk, Wear little kid pajamas

Physical Description: 5'7" humanoids with lightly colored uniforms or a bug like appearance

Indigenous peoples all over the world have been encountering aliens for hundreds of years. They are called the "Star People" and are commonly described as humanoid like beings wearing lightly colored jumpsuits. Stories of the Star People and their contact with native people were collected by investigator Ardy Sixkiller Clarke in her seminal work "Encounters With Star People", a collection of over a thousand stories of alien contact with humans. One common thread in these stories is that the Star People are usually seen after a sighting of a cigar/cylindrical shaped object in the sky resembling a fuel tank.

One remarkable Star People story is that of a Native American named Chauncy and his dog named Blue Sun. The dog began barking one evening and bolted away. Chauncy followed and found an alien standing over Blue Sun. Chauncy pulled out his shotgun and fired but the alien was unphased. He described the being as a small humanoid wearing a jumpsuit (that looked like kids pajamas) and a belt with a circular contraption. The alien, having never seen a dog, walked it to his ship and asked Chauncy "Can I have your dog?". Chauncy said no and the being left. A few years later Chauncy died and his faithful dog stood vigil at his grave, a few days later the dog disappeared!

There are hundreds of similar stories of Star People. These beings are known to have the ability to appear and disappear, use telepathic communication with humans, travel vast distances in cigar-shaped ships and steal dogs at will.

Quotes:

"Can i have your dog?"
- A Star Person

"I've had brutal ass surgery 5 times!"
- Brian Frange

Thick Kids

Episode 205: Whitley Strieber's Communion

Strengths: Space travel, Large needles, Anal probes

Weaknesses: Cinnabons, Malpractice lawsuits, Dance offs

Physical Description: 3 ½ feet tall pig-like blue doctor aliens with 2 dark holes for eyes and a black downturned line for a mouth. Wearing a uniform consisting of a smooth rounded hat and an armored vest.

Whitley Strieber was spending the Christmas holidays with his family in a cabin in upstate New York. One night, he awoke to a strange whooshing sound and saw strange beings approaching him. He was transported to a spaceship by an invisible elevator. He blacked out. When he came to, he was strapped to a table and surrounded by little blue alien doctors.

Whitley describes these being as 3 ½ feet tall pudgy blue pig monsters with two dark circles for eyes and a black upturned line for a mouth, which sometimes made an "O" shape. They wore smooth, rounded hats and an armored vest or breastplate covered their midriff. He said they looked like Big Thick Kids! The Thick Kids then showed Whitley a very large needle and he began screaming. In an effort to calm him down, a female voice asked Whitley what would make him stop screaming. He replied, "Will you let me smell you?". He then smelled them and determined that the Thick Kids smell like cardboard dipped in Cinnamon or a Cinnabon.

They inserted the needle into his head and then showed him another surgical instrument. This time they presented an enormous foot long triangular shaped object that was gray and scaly with a network of wires on the end that appeared to have a life of its own. They inserted it into his anus, he then blacked out again and woke up later in his cabin.

Quotes:

"Weather report says it's gonna snow tomorrow. Hayayy!!"
- Whitley Strieber and son

"Can you say erection?"
- Christopher Walken

Tulpas

Episode 155: Tulpas

Strengths: Created entirely in the mind, Manipulation of humans, Often very sexy

Weaknesses: Don't really exist, Created by "Bronies", Don't actually exist

Physical Description: Tulpas can take any form the creator chooses, most commonly My Little Ponies or Bigfoot.

A Tulpa is an entity created in the mind, acting independently of, and parallel to your own consciousness. They are essentially a sentient being living inside you but separate from you.

One Tulpa believer, Jacob, is what is known as a Tulpamancer and the creature he created is a pony named Aurum. "Auri" for short; is a My Little Pony character with a gray coat, purple mane and bat wings.

Jacob created his Tulpa after discovering a website through the Brony community, which he was quite active in. It was through the website Tulpa.info that the keys to the ancient art of Tulpamancy were revealed. Through a process known as "Narration", Jacob began speaking to a nonexistent imaginary friend in the hopes that they would come to life. After 2 months of talking to nothing, his new Tulpa finally replied. Jacob was overcome with joy.

Through his new relationship with an imaginary pony, Jacob became a much happier person and improved drastically in sports. His new training partner Auri would push him to excel in basketball, cross country, track and boxing. Tulpas also have the ability to possess the individual temporarily, during possession Auri can take a human form.

Quotes:

"I made her a pony, she's cool with it, it works for us" - Jacob

"This solves all my problems" - Jacob

Unarians

Episodes 256, 257 & 258

Strengths: The power and love of the entire universe. Pure unadulterated insanity. Fabulousness

Weaknesses: The limits of the human body. Space fleets that ignore earthly deadlines

Physical Description: Human in appearance, but are immortal souls. Shiny, glorious costumes representing the universe

Unarius (Universal Articulate Interdimensional Understanding of Science) was founded in 1954 in Los Angeles, CA by Ernest and Ruth Norman.

Unarians believe in immortality of the soul and that everyone has been reincarnated many times over millions of years. They also believe that our solar system was once inhabited by ancient interplanetary civilizations. The organization focuses on the tenets of love and peace, rather than using exclusionary tactics. Channeling with extraterrestrial beings allowed the Normans to direct information from the stars to useful books, TV shows, and movies for the benefit and enlightenment of all!

Ruth Norman (also known as Archangel Uriel) is the most prominently featured Unarian, and also the best dressed. Before she shed the "overcoat of humanity" in 1993, she lavishly decorated her earthly form with costumes depicting the sparkly, seizure-inducing glories of the universe.

After the deaths of the Normans and subsequent leader Charles Louis Spiegel, the organization has struggled. Another problem that the organization faces is that a scheduled space fleet that was supposed to harken "The Change" (a nicer version of the apocalypse/rapture) neglected to show up in 2001. The organization has now gone back to focusing on the books that Ernest Norman wrote and asserting that the space fleet is still coming, we just have to be patient.

Valiant Thor

Episode 123: Valiant Thor

Strengths: Baby-soft skin, Thought transference (Jedi mind tricks), Positive thinking (The Secret), Indestructible suit, Perfect English, Magic

Weaknesses: Probably just some guy who looked like a cigarette salesman

Physical Description: Tall white guy, Business suit, perfect brown hair, a Donald Draper-looking fellow or regular mobster

One of the finest leaders of the planet Venus, Val was selected by Central Control as Space Emissary to the planet Earth. (Was he really though?)

On March 16th, 1957, Valiant Thor landed in Alexandria, Virginia, and used his amazing mental abilities to gain an audience with President Eisenhower and delivered a letter with recommendations from Central Command for Earth to avoid atomic destruction. Val claimed that the Bible was a historical account and that Jesus was an alien. Val also worked with Phil Schneider's father, Oscar.

Though practical considerations prevented the full implementation of these suggestions, Val was given a beautifully furnished apartment in the Pentagon, where he lived for three years before returning to Venus.

Quotes:

"I come from the place your Bible calls The Morning Star and the Evening Star."
- Valiant Thor

"Wh-wh-what is that, Venus?"
- President Eisenhower

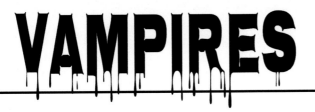

VAMPIRES

Episode 156 - Real Vampires
Episode 226 - Vampire Bones

Strengths: Powerful sense of smell, Fangs,
Super strength, Immortality

Weaknesses: Sunlight burns their insides,
Smell farts all the time, Need blood to survive

Physical Description: Pale skin, Wimpy, Fake
fangs, Long hair, Colored contacts, Long coats,
Looks like a pickup-artist

People in the middle ages believed vampires roamed the countryside sucking blood
from their victims.

In the present time, many vampires have made their way onto talk shows and
Youtube to talk about this debilitating condition.

Don The Vampire King appeared on The Tyra Banks show to talk about life as a
vampire. He successfully passed the smell test, smelling three different items with
a blindfold on and guessing what they were. He must be a vampire, right?

Another vampire appeared on Youtube going by the name of Logan. He really gave
an insight into life as a vampire. When his dad takes him to baseball games in the
sun he feels like his insides are on fire. Whenever one of his friends breaks wind
in his presence, he can smell the fart immediately and at a stronger degree than
most people.

Quotes:

"Smell It!"
- Tyra Banks

"Image that, all the time,
everywhere that you are"
- Logan The Vampire

"So you have a sensitive
smell more than the
average human, right?"
- Tyra Banks

THE VRIL

Episode 135: Body Snatching Underground Lizard People

Strengths: Descended from dinosaurs, Unlimited power, Can control humans

Weaknesses: Some are small in size, Depend on humans for food, Dumb names like Matilda and Herbert

Physical Description: Either 8 foot or 1 and ½ foot tall ancient lizards with red scales and a raised proboscis on their head. The larger Vril have long necks like a Grey Alien

The Vril are an indigenous race of lizards that have lived deep within the planet since prehistoric times. They survived the mass extinction of the dinosaurs by hiding deep within the earth. They have access to an unlimited source of energy called "Vril" that supplies all of their needs. They are a carnivorous species who love fresh human flesh.

The Vril have had contact with humans for centuries. Adolf Hitler made a deal with the Vril that gave him powerful Atlantean technology in exchange for delicious humans. According to Donald Marshall, a cloned Illuminati slave, the Vril have been in contact with royalty, religious leaders and powerful politicians for centuries. These powerful humans protect the Vril in exchange for gold and other valuable resources from deep within the Earth. These humans are also required to keep the Vril satisfied by supplying fresh people for them to consume.

There are 3 types of Vril Lizards. Type 1 are 1 ½ foot creatures with red scales and a small proboscis sticking out of their heads. Type 2 are non-parasitic and uninteresting. Type 3 are 8 ft. tall with long necks who resemble grey aliens. The most disturbing power of the Vril is their ability to send their life force into another being and have complete control over their new host. This is a process called "Sweating the Quill" in which they attach their proboscis to a person's eyeball and are able to transfer their consciousness into the selected host. Donald Marshall believes that many powerful individuals throughout history have been taken over by this fearsome species of ancient dinosaurs.

Quotes:

"Pokey Pokey Pokey"
- Donald Marshall

"Herbert...Herbert"
- Donald Marshall

WEREWOLVES and RUGARUS

Episode 250: The Cajun Werewolf Part One
Episode 251: The Cajun Werewolf Part Two
Episode 252: The Cajun Werewolf Part Three

Strengths: Speed, Super strength, Giant claws, Shapeshifting, Lent

Weaknesses: Can't count to 13, Silver bullets, Decapitation

Physical Description: Tall, furry dog-like man beast that roams the forests. Red eyes, big claws, and big teeth, all the better to hear/eat you with.

Werewolves are a legendary cryptid of the dog-man variety. Though there are tales of similar dog-men spanning the globe, their origins are most often associated with European folklore.

Hapless victims of werewolf bites can suffer the effects of transformation (in most legends this requires a full moon) and are cursed to become werewolves themselves until the original werewolf is annihilated or if the sufferer does not tell if it's wolfy secret for a year and a day. Silver bullets are an acceptable method of destruction, but decapitation is ultimately recommended.

Many sightings have been recorded in North America, with a number of these claiming that dogmen were hanging out with bigfoots, creating a hairy inter-species colony of reprobate hybrids.

In Native American legend, skinwalkers have the ability to shapeshift into werewolves (or other animals) at will.

The Rougarou is a legend specific to the swamps and bayous of Louisiana. Other similar names and spellings are Rugaru, Loop Garou, and Loop Garoup. The best way to avoid a hairy encounter with these beasts is to staunchly practice Lent or make it try to count to 13. Leaving a ton of beans on your doorstep will suffice to confuse it until help or dawn can arrive. It is acceptable to use your child as bait to lure the Rougarou so you can record it, be extensively interviewed, and post it on social media.

Quotes:

"Growled at, yannow WOOP WOOP, and they do climb trees!"

"It's a mixture of dead fish, urine, and it smells like SHIT. You know, how something dead smells?"

Witches & Voodoo Queens

Episode 141: Haunted American Cemetaries

Strengths: Cast Magic Spells, Hot Peppers and Spicy Foods Don't Bother them

Weaknesses: Easily Crushed By Rocks, Allergic To Water

Physical Description: Black pointy hat, Broomstick, Cat accessory

When most people think about witches, images are conjured up of black hats, broomsticks, warts on noses, boiling cauldrons and felines. The Salem Witch Trials occurred in 1692 where two girls accused 150 townsfolk of witchcraft.

During the witch hysteria of the 1600's, Giles Corey was critical of the witch accusations and was then accused of being a warlock. Rocks were piled on top of him for two days in order to get him to confess to his sorcery. Every time they asked him if he was a warlock, he replied "More weight."

A specific type of sorcery known as Voodoo is found in the murky bayous of Louisiana. One famous Voodoo queen, Marie Laveau, lived in New Orleans in the 1800's. A man was on trial for murder and Marie Laveau put a bunch of hot chili peppers in her mouth and then stuck them under the judge's chair. Magically the man was found not guilty and Marie Laveau was paid with a deed to a house.

If you go to the tomb of Marie and draw three X's on her tomb, she will grant you a wish. Once the wish is granted, you have to return and circle your X's.

In 2013, a vandal painted her tomb pink and then nothing happened to him, it is believed he opened up a Frozen Yogurt shop.

Quotes:

"Can you scream like a, like a...witch?" - Bobby Bare

"More weight" - Giles Corey

YAHYEL

Episode 204: Alien Contact – Interview with the Yahyel

Strengths: High mental capabilities, Space travel, Teleportation

Weaknesses: Cake (it would get them sick), Pacifist nature

Physical Description: Transcendent beings who are the byproduct of interbreeding between Gray aliens and humans.

The first contact with the Yahyel was made by a channeler named Jonathan.

The Yahyel are a hybrid race from Earth's future who have traveled back in time to contact current day earthlings and share knowledge. They are a byproduct of interbreeding between Gray aliens and humans over many generations.

They claimed that they were aboard a giant boomerang-shaped spaceship cruising through hyperspace. They also claimed that their ship was the same ship seen in the famous "Phoenix Lights" incident in 1997. The Yahyel explained that they were telepathic beings who travel mentally through the galaxy and don't actually have names. They call themselves the Yahyel because that is the sound they make when they reply to humans contacting them, "Yah Yell!". While not having the need to eat, they revealed that a leaf was grown on their ship and they just ate it for fun.

The overall message of the Yahyel is that of positivity and transcendence. To the Yahyel, all beings all beings are created with a purpose and that purpose can be defined as whatever in life brings you to your highest excitement. This excitement is not a single overarching path, but by following your excitement from moment to moment.

Quotes:

"Hello! Hello! We are the Yahyel!
We are the Yahyel! – Jonathan

"A Leaf" – Jonathan

ZETA RETICULAN GREYS

Episode 67: The Abduction of Betty & Barney Hill

Strengths: Mind control, Abduction, Telepathic, Science

Weaknesses: Get drunk off cleaning products, Ammonia is toxic to them, Smell awful, Physically weak

Physical Description: Four feet tall, large heads, large almond shaped eyes, small slit for a mouth, no visible nose and no visible ears. Long arms and fingers that reach well below their knees when standing upright.

Betty and Barney Hill pulled over on the side of the road in New Hampshire to have hot alien role-play sex and later recounted a tale of being abducted by Greys. When Betty asked where they were from, one of the aliens showed her a star map which was later discovered to be of the star system Zeta Reticuli.

They are into taking sperm, ovum, hair and other biological samples from abductees. They smell awful like sour milk, rotten meat, mildew and as Phil Schneider put it "Worse than the worst garbage can".

Their appearance is slightly more human-looking than the average grey due to the appearance of small, hard to see ear-like bumps on the sides of their heads and a tiny nose. They still have the classic large, black, wrap-around eyes on their bulbous, bald heads. They wear skin-tight silver jumpsuits that cover their entire body except for the hands and feet.

Zeta Reticulan Greys may have made the 1954 Greada Treaty with President Dwight D. Eisenhower which allowed them to abduct and experiment on humans in exchange for advanced technology.

Quotes:

The term "Unbeliever" was first introduced by a listener in The Mailbag segment of Episode 67.

Made in the USA
Middletown, DE
16 September 2018